Sudden Country

Also by Loren D. Estleman
in Large Print:

Retro
Port Hazard
Black Powder, White Smoke
White Desert
Gun Man
The Master Executioner

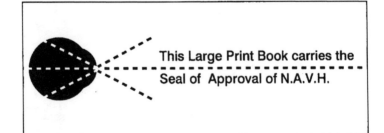

This Large Print Book carries the
Seal of Approval of N.A.V.H.

Sudden Country

Loren D. Estleman

Thorndike Press • Waterville, Maine

Published in 2005 by arrangement with Dominick Abel Literary Agency, Inc.

Thorndike Press® Large Print Western.

The tree indicium is a trademark of Thorndike Press.

The text of this Large Print edition is unabridged. Other aspects of the book may vary from the original edition.

Set in 16 pt. Plantin by Liana M. Walker.

Printed in the United States on permanent paper.

Library of Congress Cataloging-in-Publication Data

Estleman, Loren D.
    Sudden country / by Loren D. Estleman.
       p. cm. — (Thorndike Press large print westerns)
    ISBN 0-7862-7740-8 (lg. print : hc : alk. paper)
    1. Boys — Fiction. 2. Treasure troves — Fiction.
3. Large type books. I. Title. II. Series. III. Thorndike Press large print Western series.
PS3555.S84S8 2005
  813'.54—dc22   2005008455

To R.L.S.
"So be it, and fall on!"

National Association for Visually Handicapped
------------------------ *serving the partially seeing*

As the Founder/CEO of NAVH, the only national health agency solely devoted to those who, although not totally blind, have an eye disease which could lead to serious visual impairment, I am pleased to recognize Thorndike Press* as one of the leading publishers in the large print field.

Founded in 1954 in San Francisco to prepare large print textbooks for partially seeing children, NAVH became the pioneer and standard setting agency in the preparation of large type.

Today, those publishers who meet our standards carry the prestigious "Seal of Approval" indicating high quality large print. We are delighted that Thorndike Press is one of the publishers whose titles meet these standards. We are also pleased to recognize the significant contribution Thorndike Press is making in this important and growing field.

Lorraine H. Marchi, L.H.D.
Founder/CEO
NAVH

* Thorndike Press encompasses the following imprints: Thorndike, Wheeler, Walker and Large Print Press.

1

The Old Raider

I never knew my father. My mother said he died heroically fighting the Comanches at Adobe Walls, but since that battle took place two years before I was born and since my mother's favor in later years ran toward medicine drummers and goldbrickers, I came to assume he'd simply left.

I didn't resent him. The house we lived in, one of the first brick buildings in a town then called Panhandle, was ours, and its location down the street from the railroad station assured us more than enough boarders to keep us in cornmeal and homespun. By the time I was thirteen — at which point my tale begins — I had known for some little while that certain of our male roomers enjoyed more than dinner and clean sheets under our roof; and this too I accepted, unaware that the situation might be different in other households. These assignations were for the most part discreet to the point of boredom. Such, however, was not the case with Judge Constantine Blod, who came to stay with us in the spring of 1890.

My mother called him Connie when she thought I couldn't hear. He was no taller than I, with small hands and feet and a round belly that rested on his thighs when he sat, but he had the pink clean-shaven profile of a Roman senator and a crisp shelf of hair white enough for public office anywhere in Texas. He wore, in all weather, a black clawhammer coat that he spent his evenings brushing, a purple velvet waistcoat, and one of two pairs of striped trousers, the cuffs of which broke over shoes with shiny black caps and dull brown half-soles. I found none of these things compelling, but was fascinated by his rolling speech, which made a simple request for a second biscuit sound like grand oratory.

I did not become his champion until he presented me with a brace of slender novels printed on brown roughcut and bound between vermilion covers with ocher legends reading *The Morgan Gang at*

Skeleton Gulch and *Apache Dick's Last War-path, or Princess Dove-Heart's Predicament.* Both accounts were attributed to one Jed Knickerbocker. The Judge explained that Jed Knickerbocker was, in fact, himself, and that he had come west from his Manhattan townhouse in search of literary grist. I was not to share this confidence with anyone, he admonished, or risk having to entertain every lice-ridden drifter who had a tall tale to exchange for a stake. Bewildered, I agreed.

By the following day I had read both books, some parts several times. The coarse pages were filled with big men in buckskins who grappled with savage Indians and shot desperadoes, delivered eloquent addresses on fidelity and temperance, and romanced maidens with the same earnest concentration they employed lifting Apache scalps. They were called Bittercreek and Deadeye and Wild Bill, and if you called them anything else you'd better have earned the privilege or be sorry you lived long enough to meet them. When I asked the Judge if he really knew them all, he assured me of the intimacy of their acquaintance and testified that every detail was true as blue sky.

I was inclined to credit it; for I knew a

hero. Although I would not have presumed to ask Mr. Henry Knox, master of the Panhandle School where I studied, to recount his experiences in the late war, his lean moustachioed countenance and professional austerity seemed to confirm rumors I'd heard of his conspicuous performance as an officer with General Ledlie's cavalry. I suppose he was handsome, judging by my mother's embarrassingly girlish behavior whenever they met. Previously I'd assigned his lack of response to the existence of a Mrs. Knox, a pillar in the local G.A.R., and two young Knoxes in grades below mine, but now I knew that a granite reserve was part of the heroic character. I had also seen the saber hanging in the little room off the schoolroom where he disciplined pupils, against the fashion of the day, in private.

Mother's special gentlemen held no real attraction for me. They were like dim relatives of uncertain connection, and outside my notice. In that light it shames me somewhat to confess that the Judge bought me for the price of two nickel novels. I followed him everywhere, ambushing him with questions. Had he seen Apache Dick's belt woven of human hair? (He had.) Did Wild Bill still limp from the effects of the

Cheyenne lance that had transfixed his thigh? (He did not.) Was Bittercreek really a Creole from New Orleans? (He was.) What was a Creole? That he had the patience to answer each query demonstrated that he had sat still for his share of tall tales carried by lice-ridden drifters.

On the third morning after he had given me the books, I fell upon him while he was shaving over the basin in his room. He had his collar off and his galluses down and was scraping a delicate pattern around a wen on his right cheek. His rosewood toilet case lay open on the washstand, exposing a row of razors with black gutta-percha handles in slots labeled with the days of the week. I asked him what literary prospects a town like Panhandle offered.

"None at present," he said, flicking lather and bloody bits of wen into the basin; the door had startled him. "I expect that will change within forty-eight hours."

"What happens then?"

"There is a clipping from the March 18th New York *Sun* in my coat. You may examine it."

His coat hung on a portable walnut rack that had belonged to my father, the precise location of which in the house always indicated which gentleman boarder had at-

11

tracted my mother's fancy this season. Identifying the described clipping in a brittle amber sheaf of them as thick as a pocket Bible was somewhat more difficult. There were an account of a shooting in Denver as wired to the *Herald*, a grisly piece from the *World* about the discovery of an Albany alderman's body on the east bank of the Hudson River wearing the head of a woman reported missing in New Jersey in February, and sundry items from *Harper's Weekly* about the Ghost Dance hysteria among the Dakota Sioux. Finally I culled a two-inch bit printed in tiny blurred characters and bearing on one margin the word *Sun* in Judge Blod's crabbed hand, along with the aforementioned date.

MAN-KILLER FREED

Austin, Tex., March 16th — In a move considered by many to have sealed his political fate, Governor J. S. Hogg today granted a pardon releasing former Quantrill raider Jotham Flynn from the Texas State Penitentiary at Huntsville after serving twenty years of a life sentence for the murder of an Amarillo man in 1869. Flynn is believed to have participated in the Centralia massacre and the raid on Lawrence during the late war.

"Is Flynn coming here?" I asked.

"I wired him train fare in Huntsville before I left New York, with promise of further compensation if he would meet me here on the fifth. That is the day after tomorrow. I think it unlikely that he has superior prospects after two decades behind bars.

"He sounds a fair ogre."

"Bloody Bill Anderson once said that Flynn would cosh a Sister of Mercy for the gold in her molars."

I returned the clipping to his coat. Holding it had suddenly become unpleasant. "Why write of him?"

"Fodder, young Master Grayle." He splashed his face and mopped it dry, staining the towel. "It runs parlous low. The frontier is closing and most of the men of iron are east, treading the boards or performing with Cody's circus. I daresay my alacrity has snatched Flynn from beneath the whiskers of Colonel Ingram and Ned Buntline, the prevaricating sot."

"Why Panhandle and not Huntsville?"

"He has reasons for returning to this

country, the exact nature of which I cannot share at the present juncture. By making the journey possible I hope to have raised my stock with him." A twinge disturbed his noble pink features. "And now you must leave me to my own company. My old wound wants soaking."

He claimed an injury from Spotsylvania Courthouse, but even then I recognized his treatment — submerging in epsom and elevation of his swollen right foot — as identical to that of Roundtree Zimmerman, Panhandle's barber, who suffered from gout. And so it is to the common complaint of aristocrats and European monarchs that I owe everything which followed.

On the morning of the fifth, Judge Blod could not leave his room. In spite of my mother's remedies, including the abominable soup she made for shut-ins and a wondrous stack of pillows borrowed from the sofa in the parlor to support his wrapped foot, he sat lowing and comparing his misery to certain *dramatis personae* in Aeschylus and the Bard. Finally he pressed me to represent him at the depot. I was to escort Flynn back to the boarding house.

Notwithstanding my reservations concerning the man's character, I was elated, but too mannerly to show it in that sick-room. "How will I know him?"

"If you do not recognize him immediately, he is not the man I have traveled halfway across the continent to interview." And with that he subsided in his deep chair, muttering dark observations upon the death of kings.

When I arrived at the station the train was in, black and oily-smelling and hemorrhaging steam out of jets between the wheels. Passengers were departing the platform on the arms of spouses, although not many; Panhandle was not Amarillo. I felt panic. Had he stalked off, infuriated when no one was there to receive him? How many Sisters of Mercy would pay for my sloth? I asked the conductor, a long brown man with muttonchops, if anyone had alighted who had not been claimed. And then I saw Flynn.

I knew him, just as the Judge had promised. He was stepping off a rear car, one hand bent palm-up under the latigo of a big saddle polished a deep cherry color in the throat from much riding, the other steadying a blanket roll over his right shoulder so decrepit it looked as if it would crumble if he unlashed it. At first I thought he was as short as the Judge, but as he

15

came my way along the cars I saw that his knees were bent alarmingly, the toes of his broken boots turned inward cowboy fashion. He was exceptionally broad across the shoulders and wore a tattered duster over clothes of no particular color and a stained and shapeless slouch hat whose wide brim swung down across his face, exposing only full brown beard tangled with gray. I remember that as he walked he wobbled a little, turning his head from side to side as if quartering the platform, humming tonelessly, and then singing, in a deep hoarse voice, a song unfamiliar to me then, but whose lyrics and melody I would come to know like a catechism:

> *Oh, I'm a good old rebel,*
> *now that's just what I am!*
> *For this fair land of freedom.*
> *I do not care a damn!*

From that day to this I have never seen a man who appeared so obviously bereft. Even in my innocence I could see the evil he wore like a physical deformity. I stood pegged to the spot while he passed, trailing a pungent mix of sour sweat, ancient horse, and green whiskey. His back was to me when I turned at last and said, "Mr. Flynn?"

His quickness was rare in an athletic boy, astonishing in a middle-aged man who had been locked away half his life. Before the roll and saddle hit the boards he was upon me, the front of my shirt bunched in one fist, its mate grasping the handle of a knife with a blade as wide as my hand. The point pricked the underside of my chin.

I could not move. The conductor, seeing that I had located my party, had swung back aboard the train, leaving us alone on the platform. I saw Flynn's face then, for we were crowded together under the brim of his hat: two red-veined eyes with shrunken pupils set in a gray pallor, a nose that was little more than a pair of holes in a lump twisted like hemp, brown teeth with black gums grinning in a thicket of wiry hair. I saw it from a distance of two inches, my eyes watering before breath of an unholy vileness, breath of the kind that must be said to have escaped rather than been released, of rotten teeth and half-digested spirits and corruption of the soul. I felt dizzy.

"Who are you, and by whose leave do you call me by that name? Answer true, or I'll cut your tongue out the hard way." And for emphasis he deepened the knife's bite. Blood trickled into my collar.

"David — I'm David Grayle," I said. "I — my mother owns the Good Part Boarding House. Judge Blod sent me to bring you back."

I hadn't moisture in my mouth to do more than whisper, but he had no trouble hearing me at that distance. "Show me you're from Blod."

Fortunately, I had been carrying one or the other of the two Knickerbocker books doubled up in my hip pocket for almost a week. When he slackened his grip on my shirt, I scooped out *The Morgan Gang at Skeleton Gulch* and held it up in front of his face. He stared at the garish cover for close to a minute. If I'd known then that he had never learned to read I might have swooned from dread, if not from the stench of his breath. As it was, the pen-and-ink illustration of Deadeye Morgan shooting the buttons off a sheriff's vest mesmerized him long enough for his murderous instincts to subside. At length he thrust the knife into a stiff rawhide sheath on his belt.

"Hoist that saddle, boy. I been hauling it for two hunnert miles and my hand's set up."

I did as directed, using both hands and swaying under the weight. He picked up the blanket roll and we started for home.

Or so I thought. For home was but the first stop on a journey that would carry me far from familiar things.

But I am getting ahead of myself.

There is much to tell.

2

JOE SNAKE

Oh I'm a good old rebel,
now that's just what I am!
For this fair land of freedom
I do not care a damn!

I'm glad I fought against it,
I only wisht we'd won;
and I don't want no pardon
for anything I done.

Mother had prepared a room for our new
lodger across from the Judge's. It had been
occupied until lately by a young type-writer
from New Hampshire who had married her
employer and moved out, leaving behind
blue chintz curtains and a faint trace of
lemon verbena. The latter fled quickly when
Flynn unrolled his disgraceful blanket upon

the bed. He had been carrying two crockery jugs inside it, and the acrid fumes that issued forth when he slipped the knot announced that one at least had broken, probably when he'd dropped the bundle on the depot platform. Immediately the air in the room took on the aspect of Price's Saloon in Panhandle, whereupon Flynn left off singing and began cursing. He had the voice and vocabulary for it, and it would likely have continued for some time had not Mother appeared at the hall door.

She was then just two years past thirty. She always wore her hair pinned up, but not tightly, and standing with the sun behind her she seemed haloed in rosy gold. As far as a boy notices such things about his mother I was disposed to confess that the high color we shared suited her far better. I was not alone. I had once overheard Roundtree Zimmerman remarking to a customer in his barber chair that Evangeline Grayle's face and configuration had a more potent effect on him than lithographs he'd seen of the Jersey Lily. I remember it had troubled me, for I thought that my mother had been likened to a prize cow.

Her sudden appearance at that moment was sufficient to halt Flynn in mid-

21

invective. He considered her, his jaw hanging, and then he dumbfounded me by snatching off his hat. His brow was simian, his hair flat and slick like an otter's coat.

Assuming the cordial air she reserved for boarders who held no romantic interest for her, my mother introduced herself and said, "Welcome to my house, Mr. Flynn. Judge Blod has arranged for your first week's stay. Meals are served downstairs in the dining room at seven, noon, and six. I must ask that if you plan to drink in my house, you will keep your door closed."

"Yes, ma'am."

"David, the woodbox is empty."

"The Judge asked me to tell him when Mr. Flynn arrived," I said.

"I think he knows. But don't take too long about it. Mr. Flynn." She grasped the doorknob.

"Pleasure, ma'am."

For a time after we left him, Flynn was quiet. I reported his presence to the Judge, who indeed was aware of it, sitting with his foot in a steaming basin and sipping Mother's soup in a spoon. He said that he expected to be ambulatory soon and would visit his guest then. As I went out, drawing the door shut, the deep hoarse voice started up again across the hall.

I hates the Yankee nation
and everything they do.
I hates the Declaration
of Independence too!

We had a backyard that was mostly bunch grass and prairie dog holes, with a bench I had made from old barn wood where Mother sat while she peeled potatoes in the cottonwood shade. That afternoon Flynn and the Judge shared the bench. Judge Blod dug his hickory cane into the earth and made notes with a soft pencil on foolscap while the old guerrilla remembered aloud, pulling regularly at a handsome pewter flask engraved with the mysterious initials W. A., which he had evidently filled from the unbroken jug in his room. I was allowed to sit on the back porch and listen.

"Bloody Bill told Arch Clement to muster out them Yanks," he recalled. "Arch started the shooting. I reckon I finished it. Well, sir, I got to say that when the smoke lifted, them bluebellies laid straight as fence pickets. Old Abe trained 'em smart. Haw-haw." He coughed, spat phlegm, and took another pull.

"I wasn't referring to the troop train at Centralia. I meant the federal payroll train outside St. Louis in 1863." The Judge pretended to read his notes, but from my angle I could see he was watching Flynn sideways under his lashes. Flynn belched.

"I don't know that one. I was down with fever most of '63." He sang:

> *They died of Southern fever,*
> *and Southern steel and shot;*
> *and I wisht it was three million*
> *instead of what we got!*

The interviewer didn't pursue the point immediately. He spent some time exploring Flynn's relations with Captain William Clarke Quantrill and Frank and Jesse James, then left the war to examine the raider's career as a bandit during peacetime. Flynn's responses were detailed, gleefully unrepentant, and (for I must be as candid) sufficiently bloodthirsty for the ears of an impressionable boy of thirteen. Had my mother known what I was hearing, I have no doubt that her infatuation with the Judge would have been greatly strained, if not ended. In his defense I must depose that he seemed to have forgotten my presence entirely. As for Flynn, he positively enjoyed performing for a larger audience, cutting sly glances my way whenever his narrative waxed especially graphic. He became vague only when Judge Blod's probings entered the year 1863, particularly the details of the St. Louis payroll robbery, and the days immediately preceding Flynn's arrest for murder in Amarillo six years later. Whenever the conversation turned in either direction he would grow morose, renewing his assault upon the contents of the flask.

"Why did you kill Peckler?"

"Son of a bitch cheated at cards." The flask went up.

"You weren't playing cards."

"I recollected suddenlike."

"You cut out his heart with your bowie and left him bleeding on the saloon floor while you ordered another drink. He was your only friend in Texas."

"A friend don't call a friend a liar."

"You said he was a card cheat."

"That too." The flask went up.

The Judge had stopped writing moments before. He was studying Flynn openly now. "What do you hear from Black Ben?"

I have said that Flynn's face was pale — doubtless a legacy of his lifetime in Huntsville. Now it became positively colorless. His eyes smoldered like cinders on a pillowslip. Suddenly he lurched to his feet, clawed for balance, and groped for the knife on his belt. But his inebriation had dulled his reflexes and Judge Blod, quite forgetting his sore foot, leapt from a sitting position onto the porch. He nearly kicked me over.

"You are weary from your journey," he said. "I shall leave you to rest."

He retreated inside. Belatedly, I reached for the door as it was closing. Flynn's knife sprang handle-first out of the wooden frame next to my head.

"Hand me my sticker, boy."

Hoping that history was not preparing to repeat itself, I worked the blade free with difficulty and crept toward the bench. My intention was to place it there and withdraw indoors before he could move. A hand horny with old filth and callosities pinned my wrist to the bench.

"How's your eye, boy?" His breath was as rank as before, but now something new had insinuated itself, a metallic odor that if he were anyone else I should have said was fear.

I stammered that my vision was satisfactory. He held on. "Spot a stranger, would you?"

I nodded. He let go of me then, searched among his clothing as if for vermin, and produced a stained leather pouch from which he extracted a handful of notes, some new, some greasy and dilapidated, and one the color of parchment that stood out among the green-backs. He left it there, peeling a crisp dollar off the outside and holding it up. It was last year's issue and I supposed it had been given to him by the Judge.

"This here's yours," he said. "Another one for every face you see in this country you didn't before. Particular I want you to look out for a big man with a black mark on the left side of his face like branded Cain and a Judas eye. You feature that?"

"What is a Judas eye?"

"Glass, boy. With a wicked shine in it as like as if he could still see with it. It's the ones he's murdered he's looking at. You see a man who answers to that, you rabbit-run back here and tell old Flynn and there's four more of these for you Johnny-on-the-spot." He grabbed my hand just as the flow of blood was returning and crumpled the dollar into it. He closed my fingers over the note and held on. His eyes looked as if they were floating in blood. "You see someone like that and I *don't* hear it from you, I'll cut off your ears and cure them and hang them from my watch chain. You feature *that?*"

Again I nodded. He pushed me away and I mounted the porch quickly and opened the door. Before closing it behind me I glanced back and saw him rescue the pewter flask from the ground where it had fallen.

He was not at supper that evening. Judge Blod was, seated at an angle to the table with his foot supported upon a vacant chair. We had no other boarders at the time, and when Mother went into the kitchen to bring back dessert I took the opportunity to ask the Judge about Black Ben.

"Some sort of superstition among the men who rode with Anderson and Quantrill," he said, wiping his lips. "I've heard men who would cut a stranger's throat for looking at them crossly speak the name in whispers like frightened children. Still I was not prepared for the violence of Flynn's reaction. Whoever or whatever this Black Ben is or was, he does for a bogey among old nightriders."

"Do you think Flynn took part in that train robbery?"

"I think it likely. It will make an ideal subject for the book."

There was a hollowness in his words, but I was prevented from pursuing the point by Mother's return. Judge Blod retired directly after finishing a large slice of blueberry pie and I had not the opportunity to speak with him again that night. When I went up to my own room sometime later, there was a light under Flynn's door. He did not sing that night, however.

I saw the first stranger at church that Sunday.

I was not the only one who noticed him. He was quite as tall as Lloyd Weems, Panhandle's blacksmith and the tallest man in town, and nearly twice as thick through the middle, although he was not fat. His features were plainly Indian, dark as old blood with sharp black eyes crowding a nose like a bent wagon hitch, a straight line of mouth, and blue-black hair cut in a bowl. He did not go in, but stood outside the door studying each parishioner's face as it went inside. His clothes were unremarkable except for a canvas coat too heavy for the warm spring morning. I was certain it concealed a weapon.

He was gone when we filed out after the Reverend Thornharvester's sermon. Muttering some excuse to my mother about a forgotten errand, I ran ahead of her back to the Good Part and found Flynn seated alone on the bench in the backyard, gripping his flask. I blurted out my news.

"Joe Snake," he said, so low I scarcely heard him. His whiskers were on his chest and it was clear he already had a fair start on that day's measure, although it was not yet noon. "Alone, you say?"

"Just him. I think he is armed."

"He wouldn't be Joe Snake if he ain't. You wasn't followed?"

I shook my head. In truth I was not sure, for I had been too full of my mission to take note.

"Well, they mean to find me if they looked in church." He swigged whiskey. The overflow glittered in his beard. "Boy, is there a gunsmith in this town?"

"Mr. Sterner."

He set the flask down on the bench, got out his pouch, and handed me a wad of greenbacks. "Ask him has he a Navy Colt's .36. If he hasn't, a .44 Army will do. Give him his price and get powder and shot and bundle it back here pronto. Take your dollar out of what's left."

"Yes, sir." I folded the money into a shirt pocket and buttoned the flap.

"Flynn's counting on you, boy."

It was as close to civil as he had ever come with me. I said yes sir again and cut across the Fredericksons' yard next door to avoid intercepting Mother.

The pistol, shiny black with a cedar handle, had a long heavy barrel and a smooth cylinder. Mr. Sterner, whose command of English was too tenuous to phrase questions he wanted to ask, explained in broken sentences that the weapon had been converted to accept cartridges and sold me a box of them as well. I carried my purchases home in a sack.

When I opened the front door, Joe Snake was standing in the parlor beside my mother.

3

Quantrill's Gold

He looked even bigger indoors. His blue-black head threatened the ceiling, and a parlor spacious enough to allow five full-grown boarders to stretch their bones of an evening seemed scarcely to contain his barrel torso. His scent, not nearly so rank as Flynn's, but redolent of woodsmoke and worn leather, filled the corners. His coat was open and his right hand rested on the curved ivory handle of a big pistol thrust under his belt in front.

"Flynn with you?" he demanded, in a rattling whisper that seemed to explain his name.

I looked at my mother, attired in the blue dress with white ruffles and flowered hat she wore for church and still clutching her reticule. "This gentleman wishes to visit Mr. Flynn," she said. "He isn't in his room. Do you know where he went?" Her eyes flickered toward the back of the house, telling me much.

"I think he went into town," I said after a moment.

There was a silence. Then a hoarse drunken baritone drifted in from the back-yard:

Oh, I'm a good old rebel,
now that's just what I am!

As Joe Snake listened, his broad dark face divided in a horrible smile. The top part seemed to peel away from the bottom exactly in the middle, exposing grotesque teeth like crooked headstones. His head turned slowly. The big pistol came out.

I pulled the Navy Colt's out of the sack, or almost. The iron sight snagged the material and the sack dangled from the end with the box of cartridges in the bottom. I hauled back the hammer with both thumbs. It made a loud double click.

The Indian's head came back around. The awful grin vanished, but now a black emptiness opened behind his eyes. It put me in mind of fresh graves. "That gun ain't loaded."

I almost gave up then, for he was right. Then I realized that the sack concealed the empty chambers from his view, and that he was merely trying to trick me. I held on. It was not easy. Heavy to begin with, the barrel was weighted down further by the sack and its contents and wanted to pull forward and down. As I fought it, my field of fire drifted from Joe Snake's chest down to his groin and back up. Perhaps it was my saving grace. Although his own aim upon me was steady, he could not know where I would hit if the Navy went off. In spite of that, he grinned again.

"Getting heavy, uh? I bet you like to put it down. Maybe I just wait."

It was getting to be like holding a flag-staff at arm's length. My tendons ached. The smooth wooden grip grew slippery in my hands. My aim was drifting more widely. Mother was in as much danger of being shot as the Indian, or would have been if the Navy were loaded.

"Maybe I don't wait," said Joe Snake. "Maybe I just take that away from you now." He took a step forward.

Judge Blod came downstairs, buttoning his waistcoat. A stair creaked and the Indian swung around in a crouch behind the pistol. Mother hit him with her reticule.

The previous autumn she had read an article in *Galaxy* about English gentle-women who had been set upon by Irish toughs in the London Underground. Not knowing what an Underground was, but refusing to wait until the custom migrated to Panhandle, she had taken to carrying a pair of iron doorknobs in her reticule whenever she left the house. Their combined weight struck Joe Snake behind his left ear and he fell to one knee, dropping his pistol. It clattered across the hardwood floor. Mother took two steps and dropped her skirts over it.

Outside, Flynn sang:

I won't be reconstructed,
I'm better now than them;
and for the carpetbagger
I don't give a damn!

The Judge had dropped down when he saw the weapon swinging his way and re-mained crouched behind a stair rod. The Indian, still half-kneeling, shook his head like a dog, looked around for the pistol, then lurched upright and charged the open door behind me. I barely got out of his path.

In front of the house a horse screamed

and I turned in time to see Mr. Knox, my schoolmaster, drawing rein aboard his black buggy in the street. His dun mare Cassiopeia reared and pawed the air. Joe Snake picked himself up out of the dust where he had fallen almost under the horse's hoofs, ran across the street, and disappeared between John Everhorn's house and stable on the other side.

"Damnation!" shouted Mr. Knox; then, spying my mother standing behind me in the doorway, swept off his gray wideawake hat. As he was still struggling with the reins in his other hand, the gesture was impressive. "I beg your pardon, Mrs. Grayle. That fellow —"

"The thing is in hand, sir."

I looked back. Judge Blod, back on his feet, had come downstairs and retrieved Joe Snake's big pistol from where Mother had left it. Now he carried the trophy past me onto the front porch.

"A renegade, imagining he could take advantage of gentle Christians on the sabbath," he explained. "It is not the first time I have disarmed one of his tribe."

Mr. Knox finished placating Cassiopeia and climbed down from his seat. Standing on the ground in front of the porch he was at eye level with the Judge. "May I?" He held out his palm. The Judge placed the weapon in it.

"Schofield." Mr. Knox took it by the frame and turned it, revealing seven notches carved inside the grip. At length he gave it back. "My compliments, sir. Unless the man is a mountebank, you've bested a formidable foe."

"Constantine Blod — Judge, New York Superior Court, retired." The Judge inclined his head. "He would have been more formidable but for the estimable lady inside. And the boy, of course."

"Henry Knox." He put on his hat to shake the Judge's free hand and turned his scrutiny on me, including the Navy Colt's dangling forgotten at my side. The sack, still attached, rested on the floor. "If you equipped yourself for learning as well as you do for fighting, David, I wouldn't have to trouble your mother on Sunday."

I said nothing, but inside I was seething. It is no sweet thing to have stood off a murderous attack by an Indian only to be dressed down for one's schoolwork in the very next minute.

"Professor, Mr. Knox?" asked the Judge.

"Schoolteacher, Judge Blod." The smile beneath his moustaches was deprecating.

"Yet a military man, from your bearing."

"I had the honor to serve the Army of the Potomac."

Behind the house, Flynn sang:

I hates the glorious Union
'tis dripping with our blood!
I hates the striped banner,
I fought it all I could.

"What in thunder is *that?*" demanded Mr. Knox.

"My guest, I'm afraid." Mother's hand smoothed the hair on the back of my head, a gesture she made only in the presence of Mr. Knox. "Judge, the Federicksons will complain."

"I shall require assistance. Mr. Knox, I find it distasteful to prevail." The Judge sounded hopeful.

Mr. Knox mounted the porch, towering there. Although he was not as tall as Joe Snake, his leanness and straightness of spine always made him appear to be looking down as from a great height. "Head or feet, Judge Blod?"

"Feet, Mr. Knox. The spirit is willing, but the back is weak." I noticed that he made no mention of his "wound," or indeed, in Mr. Knox's discriminating presence, of service in the war. The incident of

38

Joe Snake, whose pistol now reposed beneath the Judge's waistcoat, had done much to dislodge the scales from my eyes.

It did not quite come to carrying, although it might as well have. Flynn was nearly unconscious on the bench when the pair hoisted him to his feet and, supporting him unevenly with his arms slung across their shoulders, half-dragged him inside. I held doors and moved furniture out of hazard's way while they trundled him toward the staircase. At the bottom he came to himself and grasped the newel post, demanding to know what son of a bitch had stolen his flask. Mr. Knox nodded sharply over the old raider's shoulder and I fetched the item from the bench where we had left it. Flynn snatched it from me, swallowed what remained of its contents, and allowed the procession to continue, singing:

> *Three hundred thousand Yankees*
> *is stiff in Southern dust!*
> *We got three hundred thousand*
> *before they conquered us!*

When at last they descended, minus Flynn and mopping their faces, I had finished setting places for us all in the dining room. Mother served chicken and dumplings and biscuits with butter that melted into pools in the steaming insides when we spread it. I'd noticed the Judge trying to dissemble his limp on the way to the table, most likely to avoid a last-minute substitution of Mother's sickroom soup. All of his many deceptions had suddenly become apparent to me.

"Now, what was that about?" asked Mr. Knox, when we were all seated with heaped plates in front of us.

"I did not care for the man's manner," said Mother, spreading her napkin in her lap. "I do not care overmuch for Mr. Flynn's either, but he is a guest in my house and I will have no one come to harm in it. David, remove that horrible thing from the table at once. How did you come to have it in the first place?"

I got up to transfer the Navy Colt's and sack of ammunition from the table where I had placed them to a drawer of the china cabinet. "Mr. Flynn sent me to purchase it."

"Guns are no fit things for a parlor," she said. "If we had law here we would have no need for them."

Mr. Knox buttered a piece of biscuit the size of his thumbnail. It looked like something a former cavalry officer would do.

40

"The nearest law is in Amarillo. That fellow could be halfway to Mexico City by the time it arrived. Who is this man Flynn?"

Judge Blod told him. Mother's nostrils pinched, "I was not aware of his past when I allowed you to invite him here. David, were you?"

I fidgeted; for the Judge had made me a conspirator in the secret. Mr. Knox rescued me.

"That is hardly of consequence now," he said. "However, I think that Mrs. Grayle deserves to hear the tale."

Judge Blod, plainly chagrined, set down his fork and touched his lips with the napkin he had tucked into the *v* of his waistcoat. He had made a decision.

"Very well. In February of 1863, President Lincoln, threatened with a general strike among federal troops campaigning in Missouri, authorized a special payroll shipment to Springfield. A band of Quantrill's raiders under the command of Bloody Bill Anderson stopped the train outside St. Louis, slaughtered the guards, and according to accounts rode off with one hundred and fifty thousand dollars in gold double eagles. The paymaster, Captain Orrin Peckler, was wounded but survived.

41

"An expedition to capture the raiders and recover the gold ended in failure when investigating troops were unable to find tracks left by the wagon that would have been required to carry away the booty. Some time passed before it was decided that the gold had not been carried away at all, and that it had not been put on the train to begin with. By then Captain Peckler had vanished, having recuperated at his home while on leave and taken flight. Although rewards were offered for his capture, nothing was heard from him until he was killed in Amarillo four years after the hostilities ended."

"Flynn!" I cried. My meal was growing cold.

"Just so. Flynn was one of the raiders who struck the train to cover Peckler's embezzlement and share in the proceeds. Only instead of sharing, Peckler reclaimed the gold from wherever he had hidden it and fled alone. Perhaps getting wounded had turned him against his accomplices; perhaps he'd planned to cross them from the beginning. In any case Flynn caught up with him in a saloon. They quarreled, Flynn eviscerated Peckler, was arrested and tried for the crime of murder and sentenced to Huntsville. This is scarcely table

42

conversation," he said in an apologetic tone to my mother. She appeared quite as enthralled as the rest of us.

"Do you think he knows where the gold is?" I asked.

"If so he would have been long gone before the authorities came looking for him. My theory is he drank too much, lost his head, and slew Peckler before he learned the gold's location. I suspected I was on the right track when he agreed to meet me here on the apron of Amarillo after his release. From what I have observed of his conduct since his arrival I am convinced of it."

Mr. Knox deftly sculpted the meat off the leg bone in front of him with his knife. "Then why meet with him at all?"

"His story is the only gold that interests me. I am a journalist, not an adventurer."

"Dumplings, Judge." Mother offered him the bowl. After studying her face he declined.

"Where does the Indian feature?" asked Mr. Knox.

"Joe Snake ran with Flynn and some of the rest after the war. Evidently a number of his old compatriots think he knows something."

I said, "Bloody Bill?"

"Anderson and Quantrill were both killed in the fighting. But the men they trained have been leading the law a merry chase for a quarter century."

"The man with the Judas eye."

"What's that?" The Judge stared at me.

"Something Mr. Flynn said," I replied. "He told me to watch for strangers. In particular I was to look out for a big man with a black mark on his face and a glass eye. He called it a Judas eye."

"It could be anyone. Precious few of those night riders emerged unscathed from the carnage."

Mr. Knox finished his chicken and pushed his plate away. "Come, Judge. As I understand it, war booty is in the public domain. Surely it's no sin to covet an honest fortune."

"The thought has crossed my mind. What of it? If Flynn knew where to look for the gold he would not be loitering here."

"You said yourself he has been drunk since he arrived."

"True. Peckler married a Mexican woman in Amarillo, but she died several years ago. If she knew his secret it died with her."

"Perhaps Flynn doesn't know that," Mr. Knox said.

"Perhaps not." He seemed loath to agree.

Mr. Knox looked at my mother. "It is my opinion this fellow won't be back today. Rachel and the children are visiting her parents in Illinois. I think I should spend the night here in case he returns after dark."

Mother beamed.

The Judge glared.

Upstairs, Flynn sang:

> *Oh, I'm off for the frontier*
> *soon as I can go.*
> *I'll prepare a weapon*
> *and stomp on Mexico!*

4

Riders of the Night

If I had hopes that the morning's excitement would make Mr. Knox forget about my execrable record in arithmetic and geography, they were dashed quickly. After he had conferred with my mother I found myself alone in my bedroom with the problem of how many apples remained in Jeff's possession after Susan had plundered his store and ten pages in my composition book awaiting my reflections upon the annual mean rainfall in Argentina. By that time Mr. Knox had gone, to return at dusk carrying a valise. During supper I endured an oral quiz in long division while Judge Blod, uncharacteristically silent, busied himself with biscuits and gravy. Flynn did not show himself, but remained in his room, snoring rippingly and occasionally singing in his sleep about bloody banners,

sacred ground, and Mr. Lincoln's anteced-
ents.

I lay awake for some time after retiring,
partly because of Joe Snake and thoughts
of Quantrill's gold and partly because my
schoolmaster occupied the room next to
mine. A shaft of milky moonlight fell upon
my half-completed geography assignment
on the writing table, throwing a shadow
that resembled Mr. Knox, rampant on a
field of fleurs-de-lis.

If I slept at all, I had awakened by the
time a harness ring jingled directly beneath
my window. Notwithstanding Mother's
lectures about the harmful properties of
night air, I was in the habit of sleeping with
the window partially open, and the noise
carried. I might have put it down to my
imagination, which was strongest when I
lay alone in the dark on the edge of sleep,
and drifted off, had not a horse then
stamped and blown in the chill spring
night. Hard on that I heard voices.

"I see you're still carrying Bloody Bill's
flask, Flynn."

"Hell, Beacher, you know old Flynn'd
suck the sap out of a old piss-elm iffen it
was that or water."

"Where's the swag, Flynn?"

Two of the voices were unfamiliar to me.

The first had a medium quality, not harsh like Flynn's, almost pleasant. The second was a nasal whine and employed some kind of backwoods dialect that made the words nearly incomprehensible. But it was the third speaker who brought me out of bed as suddenly as if something had scurried across me in the dark; for I recognized the rattling whisper of Joe Snake.

The window overlooked the backyard. Through it, I saw Jotham Flynn standing bowlegged under the cottonwood with his back toward me, holding aloft the lamp from his room. In its light he was surrounded by four men on horseback. Their hats hid their faces, but the Indian's huge frame was obvious astride a buckskin that was too small for him so that his boots nearly touched the ground. One of the others sat a pretty strawberry roan, which shied when a third man aboard a shaggy, ill-kept bay directed a glittering stream of tobacco juice at the roan's left forefoot.

"Bull's-eye!" he said, in the nasal whine, which I have already described.

The man on the roan cursed. "Spit on your own transportation, Pike." His was the pleasant voice.

The fourth man straddled a big blaze-face which stood in my mother's flowerbed, munching on the irises she had been laboring over for three years in a place where everyone said irises could not live. He was almost Joe Snake's size but did not look as freakish because of his choice of mounts. I saw pistols in belts and holsters and saddle rifles and, in the to-bacco-spitter's hands, a bullwhip doubled over with a butt as big around as my wrist. He kept smacking his left palm with it when he wasn't despoiling the yard with his evil juice.

"Where's the swag, Flynn?" Joe Snake repeated.

Flynn laughed, coughed, and tipped up the flask he was never without. I recall wondering if the jug in his room had a bottom. "I had it, you think I'd still be here looking at your ugly face, you dumb red-skin?"

The bullwhip cracked. The flask sprang from Flynn's hand and landed with a clank in darkness. He cursed and almost dropped the lamp. He shook his stinging hand.

The man on the blaze-face said some-thing in a low voice. Pike spat, gathered in his whip, and said petulantly, "I was just practicin'."

"You wouldn't be back here you didn't

know something, Flynn," said Beacher, the man on the roan. "You remember what the Cap'n said about greed busting up all the best outfits."

"I'm writing a book is what I'm doing here." Flynn worked his fingers.

Pike laughed nastily. "You couldn't write your own name in the snow."

Joe Snake said, "I say we take out an eye."

"The right one," said Pike, turning toward the man on the blaze-face. "Then him and you could side each other."

Flynn drew his big knife. "Which one of you sons of whores is man enough to try old Flynn?"

Pike raised his whip. Flynn lunged, slashing through the man's reins. The bay backed up and tried to rear. Dropping the whip, Pike grabbed for the harness. Joe Snake meanwhile drew a carbine from his saddle scabbard and worked the lever. Flynn dashed the lamp at the buckskin's feet. It shattered, spraying flame. The horse screamed and bucked and plunged. Joe Snake fired wild, tried to hold on with one hand, lost his grip and his seat, and fell to the ground, releasing the carbine. His left foot was twisted in its stirrup. The buckskin bolted, dragging the Indian shrieking through the blaze. More shooting broke out. Flynn fell.

The house came alive. I heard the door to Mr. Knox's room crash against the wall as it was torn open, heard the Judge demanding in stentorian tones what in thunder was coming to pass. Feet pounded the staircase going down. I held my post at the window. In the light of the flames I saw the man on the blaze-face dismount and approach Flynn on the ground with a pistol in his hand. His horse shied from the burning grass but appeared otherwise unaffected by it or by the other horses' panic. Beacher had one hand on his roan's traces and the other on the harness of Pike's shaggy bay, helping him bring the animal under control. Joe Snake's buckskin was gone, leaving behind a motionless flaming something lying on the ground several yards away from the original fire. The man who had stepped down from the blaze-face turned over Flynn's body with a foot, then put the pistol away in his clothes and bent over the body. The back door banged open. He straightened, glanced that way, and retreated toward his horse. In a flash he had gained the saddle, wheeled the animal, and galloped off, shouting something unintelligible over his shoulder. Beacher left off Pike's bay and whipped the roan after the blaze-face. Pike followed, hunched over the bay's neck as he hung on to the harness. Someone discharged a firearm in the yard and I thought I saw Pike jerk as if hit, but then darkness swallowed up horse and rider.

These details remain as vivid in my memory forty years later as they appeared that night, and even though I am no more certain of the exact chronology than I was immediately afterward, I have only to close my eyes to see one in particular. When the man to whom the blaze-face horse belonged glanced toward the house, light from the fire in the yard glinted off something bright in the shadow of his face. Without doubt it was a glass eye.

"His neck is broken."

By the time I reached the back door, Mr. Knox had put out the fire smoldering in Joe Snake's clothes with one of my mother's blankets, which remained draped across the body he was examining. I could go no farther because of Mother's hands on my shoulders. I stood barefoot in my nightshirt on the threshold, smelling smoke and spent powder.

Judge Blod upended the well bucket over the last of the burning grass and joined

Mr. Knox. He had pulled on a pair of his striped trousers under his own nightshirt and thrust his feet into purple velvet slippers with worn tassels. "It must have happened when his head struck the base of the bench." With his good foot he nudged that item, which had collapsed when a leg had broken.

"Very likely." Mr. Knox stood and deposited a small pistol in a pocket of his robe. "What about Flynn?"

"Shot through the heart."

Mother's fingers dug into my flesh.

"They were after the gold," I said. "I heard them talking."

Both men stared at me. I related what I had heard. "Did you see any of them clearly?" the Judge demanded.

I shook my head. "The one with the pretty horse was called Beacher. He called the other one Pike, the one Mr. Knox shot."

Mr. Knox said, "You saw him hit?"

"I think so. He jerked in his saddle."

"Charlie Beacher and Nazarene Pike. I thought it was Pike when I saw the whip." It lay on the ground near the Judge. "The Yankee scalps that pair took would reach from here to Gettysburg."

"Really, Judge." But Mother's scolding

lacked conviction in that place.

"What about the fourth man?" Mr. Knox asked me.

"He had a blaze-face horse. No one called him by name and I couldn't see or hear him well. I think he started to go through Mr. Flynn's pockets." In my excitement I had forgotten about the glass eye.

"Looking for what, I wonder." Standing over Flynn now, Mr. Knox stroked his moustache. "I wonder as well what Flynn was doing out here with a lamp."

"He wasn't looking for his flask," the Judge said. "He had that earlier."

"I know what it was." I freed myself from Mother's grasp and turned inside.

Mother was soothing Mayellen Fredrickson from next door on the front threshold when I came downstairs fully dressed minutes later. Mrs. Fredrickson was wearing a lavender percale robe cut for a younger, less abundant Mrs. Fredrickson and fanning herself with a lace handkerchief that was plainly inadequate for anything but fanning. Mother made sympathetic sounds and closed the door firmly in her visitor's face. The night's incidents would fuel conversation at Mrs. Fredrickson's First Tuesday At Home for

54

years. Mr. Knox and Judge Blod were there as well. I held out the crumple of notes Flynn had given me that morning, less what I'd spent on the Navy Colt's and cartridges. The Judge grabbed it before Mr. Knox could move.

"There are but a few dollars here," he said, disappointed.

"He must have forgotten the errand he sent me on. I hadn't a chance to return what was left. Perhaps he thought he'd dropped them."

"What's that yellow note?" Mr. Knox asked.

"Mr. Sterner refused to accept it."

The Judge separated it and studied it at arm's length. "A Confederate five. It must have been a keepsake. It's worthless."

"It has writing on it." Mr. Knox took it from him.

Mother and I crowded in for a look; or at least that was my purpose. She rested long fingers on Mr. Knox's sleeve. On one end of the note, next to the portrait of Jefferson Davis, a number of marks had been made with a pencil. They were blurred but still discernible, and resembled nothing so much as a child's game of tic-tac-toe.

"It is a map of some kind," declared Mr. Knox.

"Quantrill's gold!" I cried.

"Balderdash. Mere doodles." Judge Blod snatched at the note, grasping only empty air as Mr. Knox turned toward me.

"Did Flynn give you this in the backyard?" he asked. I nodded. He stroked the parchment thoughtfully. "Obviously a mistake, as he could not hope to purchase anything with a Confederate note. When he discovered it was missing he went out to see if he'd dropped it in the yard and found his old friends waiting for him."

"Let us find the gold," I said.

"Let us wire the authorities in Amarillo about the dead men behind the house. There is nothing here to tell us this will direct us to gold. Even if it did, where would we begin looking? What is this 'Harney' scribbled in here? It could be in Africa or China for all we know."

"Or Argentina," said I, morosely.

"It is a mountain in South Dakota."

We all looked at Judge Blod, whose normally proud face and posture now presented a study in defeat.

"I suppose we must be confidants," he said. "Orrin Peckler had a daughter, now aged twenty-one. After her mother's death she moved from Amarillo to New Jersey, where I interviewed her. She informed me that her father was prospecting extensively in the Black Hills at the time he married her mother. When the treaty of Fort Laramie banned white men from the Black Hills in 1868, they came to Texas, where he established a freight company. It is my considered opinion that he went into that country to put gold in, not take it out."

"Why there?" asked Mr. Knox.

"Where better? The Black Hills were sacred to the Sioux, who were then at their apogee. Who better to guard his wealth until it was safe to spend, if not ten thousand savages? He had risked his life for the gold once; why not twice, in order to conceal it safely?"

"The Sioux have been on reservations for years," Mr. Knox pointed out. "What has prevented you from going in and removing the gold?"

"I had only a general location and my own suspicions. I was convinced that Flynn had the finer details but lacked the general location. Evidently he liberated Peckler's body of the note, which made an ingenious map as no one is likely to question the presence of just another war souvenir among his effects and he was not likely to spend it by mistake. But I had to wait for Flynn's release in order to see his cards."

"The map was in his possession all that time?"

"In the property room in Huntsville, to be precise. With the exception of firearms, prisoners' personal belongings are held for them and returned at the end of their sentences. However, the information was useless without a place to start. I hinted to him in my wire that I had it; that and train fare were sufficient to bring him here. He was cautious, but I fancy I was battering down his defenses when this happened."

"Forgive me for practicing similar caution. Why are you telling us this now?"

Judge Blod spread his tiny, well-kept hands. By degrees he had come back around to his orator's stance. "I am but one man, and the Black Hills are vast. This Ghost Dance business in South Dakota cannot be overlooked. I require a partner who has proven himself dependable in dangerous circumstances."

"Are you suggesting an expedition?"

"I have come two thousand miles to organize it."

Mr. Knox scowled at Jefferson Davis. "This fellow Snake must have followed Flynn here from Huntsville. After this morning's debacle he sent for help. That means the others were not far away. There may be more."

"There are more. Fifteen men stopped that Union train. Joe Snake joined the band after the war. Of the original number, five were dead before tonight and three in prison. Flynn's death leaves six. They will undoubtedly find reinforcements. We will have to move fast, before they regroup."

"I cannot close the school before Wednesday, when the spring planting break begins."

"I shall require that much time to arrange for men and supplies in Amarillo. You can meet me at the Palo Duro Hotel."

"I haven't said I'm going. We are both too old to go galloping off after buried treasure."

"Rocking chairs cost money."

"Who will look after Mrs. Grayle and David in the event the night riders return?"

"I am going on the expedition," I said.

"My room is paid up through next week," the Judge said. "Unless Evang— Mrs. Grayle has objections, you may stay there until the end of the session. After that, perhaps Mrs. Grayle has friends or family who will put them up. These dastards will quit this country soon enough when they sense their quarry has flown."

"I am going on the expedition," I repeated.

"I have a boarding house to run," said Mother.

Mr. Knox said, "Soon the Texas climate will be too hot and windy for visitors. You will not be losing much business and your safety would be a comfort to me."

Mother softened, as she always did before a masculine entreaty. "I have cousins in Amarillo. Will you escort us?"

"I shall be delighted."

I said, "If you don't take me to Dakota I shall tell everyone I know about the gold."

Judge Blod grew imperious. "Madam, your son wants discipline."

"My son's discipline is no concern of yours," Mother said coldly. "Mr. Knox, you must concur that the events of this day have entitled the Good Part Boarding House to an equal share in the reward for the gold's recovery."

"I do."

"Since we have an interest, I should like to propose my son's services as an extra to help out on the expedition."

He appeared surprised. "There will be danger."

"He will be more of a danger to himself if left behind. David is headstrong and in need of tempering. If he becomes a burden you may send him home and we will consider our agreement terminated."

"We are no nannies," protested the Judge.

"We would not have this map but for David." Mr. Knox handed me the note. "I can be no less trustful than the late Mr. Flynn."

I folded it carefully with the map inside and buttoned my shirt flap over it. "It is safe with me." Inside I was soaring.

"At the very least your geography should improve," commented Mr. Knox.

5

The Man with the Judas Eye

State of Texas
County of Carson
We the jury summoned to appear
Julius Honyocker United States Marshal and Louis Calfine Coroner the
seventh day of April 1890 to inquire
into the circumstances attending the
deaths of Jotham Flynn, transient, and
unidentified Indian male do upon our
oaths say that they came to their
deaths at Panhandle Carson County
Texas on the sixth day of April 1890
from the effects of a gunshot wound
and a bad fall on the property of
Evangeline Grayle, widow. That said
deaths were the result of a prior griev-

ance unknown to this court.
Witness our hands (etc.)

That was the way they recorded it in a thin sheath of yellow typewritten sheets that is now in my possession. I did not testify at the inquest and neither did Judge Blod, who was in Amarillo that day, having sworn to a deputy marshal named Noles or Knowles that he had slept through the incident. Mother and Mr. Knox presented the details they had witnessed, leaving out mention of the gold, which was not precisely committing perjury because they were never asked about it. The entire proceeding did not take twenty minutes.

Joe Snake could not be identified by name without further explanation and so was buried without ceremony or a marker in Stranger's Corner. Mother used the money the Judge had given her for Flynn's stay to bury the old raider in a graveside service conducted by the Reverend Thornharvester and attended by her, six elders who acted as volunteer pallbearers, and myself. She gave the greenbacks I had left after purchasing the Navy Colt's to Ovid Thanapopoulis to cut the headstone. It is there yet, reading:

JOTHAM FLYNN
D. April 6. 1890
"I'M A GOOD OLD REBEL"

Her loyalty to her boarders even in death remained a subject of much debate in Panhandle for years, including speculations I will not dignify by including here.

The last three days before the spring planting break stretched eternally for a boy who had had his first taste of adventure and the promise of more courses to come. The night riders did not return during that time, Mr. Knox remained deaf and blind to my mother's unsubtle advances and kept to the Judge's old room nights, and I longed to be away. What value the Palmer Method and the Pythagorean Theorem, when guerrilla gold beckoned? When, precisely at three o'clock Wednesday afternoon, Mr. Knox dismissed the session at last, I was so full of the expedition that I did not protest even to myself the assignment to read Mr. Dickens's *The Old Curiosity Shop* before classes resumed in May.

Mother, Mr. Knox, and I rode the train to Amarillo, where he hired a trap to convey her and her bags to the home of Cousin Gertrude, a woman of substantial presence and girth whom I could not stand. I ached with impatience. I had been to the city many times before, and apart from the release offered by any excursion outside Panhandle, I was no more taken with the place than I was with Gertrude's obfuscatory greetings and farewells. Its crooked streets and faceless buildings did not differ significantly from those of my home, albeit covering a larger area, and as is so often the case with cities isolated by great distances, its inhabitants tended to look upon visitors from smaller settlements as rubes and gawkers. Certainly we drew our share of condescending attention from passersby as Mother embraced me on the woodwalk in front of Gertrude's iron fence.

"Come back," she said.

She added nothing, for she was never effusive about those things that counted highest with her. I noticed then, standing very close to her, that we were the same height. The fact had not occurred to me before, although it has many times since; and when I think of her now I see her as she appeared that day, with her hair up and ringed in sunlight and her eyes dark and dry in the high color of her face.

Presently Cousin Gertrude came out to kiss Mother and then envelop and slobber over me. I carried the bags inside, endured more of the same, and returned to the trap, too polite to wipe my face until we were away down the street. Mr. Knox, clucking at the team and watching me out of the corner of his eye, took the wrong meaning.

"The homecoming will be sweeter for the bitterness of departure," he said.

We found Judge Blod holding court in a wingback chair in the foyer of the Palo Duro Hotel, illustrating with the tip of his cane a bloodcurdling story for a bored clerk behind the desk and a pair of loiterers who had evidently come in just to use the cuspidor. The Judge was decked out in his clawhammer and waistcoat, with a straw planter's hat whose wide brim made his face look like wicker when the light shone through it. His eyes were as bright as steel bearings.

"And that, gentlemen," he concluded, "is the story you did not read in the journals of how Deputy Marshal Murdock brought the Mercy brothers singlehandedly to their end."

"Horseshit, Judge. They was all three backshot. I seen it in *Jack Rimfire's Own*." One of the loiterers gonged the cuspidor. That reminded me of Nazarene Pike; but it was not his voice.

"Believe what you will. Posterity will have it different. And now I must take my leave of your August company, for my associates have arrived."

"What have you been doing besides stretching blankets?" Mr. Knox asked, when the Judge struggled to his feet to shake hands. The loiterers had wandered toward the staircase, most likely in hopes of glimpsing a petticoat descending.

"You catch me at rest for the first time since my arrival," said the Judge. "I've been these three days seeking volunteers. It seems no one is eager to visit the Black Hills as long as this Ghost Dance travesty continues, and I am determined not to mention gold lest we share it with half of Texas." His tone was uncharacteristically low.

"Why not wait until we reach Cheyenne?" asked Mr. Knox.

"I hope to enlist a guide and men seasoned to the country there. However, the picking will be better if we are not merely two middle-aged men and a boy when we arrive. We require men of iron to attract men of iron."

"What progress have you made?"

"I was coming to that. It is either my great good fortune or my curse to have made the acquaintance of someone who boasts a knowledge of the country where we are headed and has offered his assistance in rounding up men at arms. He is a frontiersman himself, and no greenhorn at Indian fighting, should it come to that."

"What does he want?"

"Merely a place with the expedition. He has wearied of the sedentary life, he says, and longs to return to the wide open spaces."

"Surely he has had many opportunities, if he is as experienced as you say."

"Alas, he is no longer young, and disabled besides; but not in such a way that it would hinder either our aims or our progress. He claims to speak the Sioux tongue and wishes to place himself at our service as interpreter."

"This country is full of men who say they can do things they cannot."

"Just so. To hear the man, he scouted for Custer at the Washita and Crook at the Rosebud and captured Geronimo all alone with his bare hands. In his defense, I must say that it is well-nigh impossible to call him a liar in his presence. If he is not the genuine article he ought to be."

"I would meet him."

"And so you will. He operates the

Golden Gate Saloon down the street. Perhaps you saw it on your way in."

Mr. Knox looked dubious. "A saloonkeeper?"

Judge Blod shrugged elaborately. "If you lusted after the strenuous life, would you not establish a place where those who live it yet might gather and share stories?"

"*I* would live the life. But I am able and not yet old."

The Judge directed the clerk to send our bags up to his suite and we repaired down the street to a clapboard shack of pioneer vintage with a plank nailed across the front reading THE GOLDEN GATE in Old English letters that had once been gilt, but which had since darkened and flaked away. In places only the faded wood where the paint had once been still rendered the sign legible. The front window was opaque with dust and smoke discoloration, and one of the batwing doors sagged on a cracked leather hinge. As we approached it, a man in a shapeless felt hat and dirty bib overalls hurtled through, caught his toe on the woodwalk, and fell facedown in the dust and manure of the street. A big man wearing a striped shirt and red galluses and garters came out and stood over him.

"Who cut the balls off Johnson's

bluebellies, you Yankee-loving bastard?" he demanded, and turned back toward the doors. He spied the Judge and stopped.

"Not entirely auspicious," declared the Judge; "but a meeting nonetheless. Mr. Henry Knox, it is my distinct, if peculiar pleasure to present Mr. Benjamin Franklin Wedlock, originally of Independence, Missouri."

"Your humble servant, sir," said the big man, inclining his fair head, which was as broad as any ox's. "Or so my sainted mother taught me to say in social solutions."

These I think were the first words I heard him say. My memory of them is not clear, for I was much more attentive to his appearance than to his speech. He had regular, if aging features — somewhat pale, and clean-shaven but for broad burnsides following the curve of his high cheeks. However, the skin on the left side of his face appeared to have been badly burned sometime in the distant past, for although it was smooth and not at all scarred, it was stained dead black in a patch as large as a man's hand. Even so, it was not this that transfixed me, but rather the pale blue eye on that side of his face, a fixed flat thing that did not move when its mate moved, and which was plainly made of glass.

6

Lead Flies at the Golden Gate

"Speak up, son. It is ungentlemanly to stare." Knox's words alerted me to the fact that I had been addressed by Wedlock, who was looking down at me now with his good eye turned my way and a guarded smile that showed an even row of white teeth. Still I said nothing. The artificial orb glittered in its ebony setting.

"It's the eye he's studying on," Wedlock said, good humor in his tone. "I'm used to it."

"That does not excuse the behavior," said Mr. Knox.

"How did that happen?" I demanded.

"Master Grayle!" Judge Blod began to apologize for my rudeness. Wedlock cut him off.

"The story repeats well. But it ain't for the street. Our throats would all bear sluicing on a day like this, I'll warrant." He opened one of the batwings and held it.

Mr. Knox pointed at the man lying in the dirt, who had begun to stir. "What about that fellow?"

"An insult to my hospitality. He spoke unkindly of General Lee."

"I fought for the Union myself."

"But with respect for your enemy, I'm bound. This heap of stinking guts stayed home and sold shoddy. Because of him our boys fought in rags and he had the poor judgment to call them tramps."

"They did not fight like tramps," said Mr. Knox.

"Sir, you do an old campaigner's heart proud."

The interior of the establishment was cool and dark after the hot glare of the street. It was nearly full at that early hour and an umbrella of smoke hung under the rafters. The air smelled of liquor and damp sawdust and the sour proximity of unwashed men. Behind the bar, over a mirror bearing a lumber firm's advertisement, hung a tattered Confederate swallowtail and a rusty print of Robert E. Lee in an oval frame, the only decorations in the room. Wedlock directed a lean sallow bartender dressed like himself to draw three beers and a ginger beer and carried them to a corner table in back, two mugs to each hand. We sat.

"I was privileged to serve General Jackson at Second Manassas," Wedlock said. "We fit from midafternoon until well past dark and I lost a good horse. McClellan and Banks was in retreat at midnight. The mount I drew to replace old Deuteronomy was skittish and backed up from this here bluebelly — beg pardon, Mr. Knox. Federal — corpse, and I was busy with the reins when that corpse stood up and emptied its Springfield at my face. Wasn't quite through dying, it seems. Well, I was lucky. In the heat of fighting he'd recharged that gun but forgot the ball and all I got was this here powder burn and a hole in my head where the eye was. I wore a bandanna over it through Appomattox and after the war I bought me this eye you see from a china merchant named Melander in St. Louis. It was made in Dresden."

"It is a fine thing," said Judge Blod, who for once seemed at a loss for a prettier phrase.

"What became of the man who shot you?" asked Mr. Knox.

"I had my saber. He wasn't the first man to lose his head in battle." He swallowed half his beer.

"Are you sometimes called Black Ben?" I asked.

"Master Grayle!"

Wedlock gazed at the ceiling with his working eye. The other remained on me. "Not to my face, for certain, or in my hearing. There's them that call a man all manner of things when his back is to them, so I cannot say no and swear to it. Why?"

"I was told by a man who had ridden with Quantrill to watch out for a man with a black mark on the left side of his face and a Judas eye. The name Black Ben frightened him."

"Quantrill, you say? The butcher. You keep interesting company, lad."

"I saw the man who told me that killed. One of the men who did it rode a big blaze-face and had a glass eye."

Judge Blod said, "The boy has an imagination. Pay him no heed."

"I steer clear of horses that ain't all one color," said Wedlock. "They're sore luck."

"You are not an admirer of Captain Quantrill?" Mr. Knox was studying him closely.

"Captain by whose authority but William Clarke Quantrill's? I did not join the War for Southern Independence for his like."

The strength of his feelings was evident in his tone. I was perplexed. "Are there many men who lost eyes during the war?"

"Eyes, ears, limbs — I know of one who gave half his skull to a mortar round and walked about for two years afterwards with his brains showing. Until I left Virginia for good in '66 a whole man was looked upon with suspicion." He lifted his mug. "To the maimed and dead — and them that might as well be." He drank.

"Virginia, you say." Mr. Knox set down his beer. "Judge Blod said Missouri. I hear it in your speech."

"You've sharp ears. My mother took me from Independence at a young age to live with *her* mother in Roanoke. My father was addicted to strong liquor and answered most questions with his good right hand. I was reared by women from the time I was seven until I turned sixteen and left home. Mind that never happens to children of yours."

I knew his meaning. In spite of myself I had begun to warm to the big frontiersman.

Mr. Knox said, "You told Judge Blod

you speak Sioux. Where did you learn it?"

"After the war I took work hauling freight in Nebraska. One day the train was set upon by a band of Red Cloud's warriors. I am the only survivor. An arrow through my short ribs pinned me to a wagon and I'd of got clubbed to death just like the others if I didn't think to reach up and pluck out my eye in front of them savages and stick it back in. Well, sir, that there was big medicine. They taken me back to the village and patched me up and there I stayed, eating dog and dispensing advice, until I was fit enough to make my escape. I picked up the lingo meantime, together with a fair knowledge of injun ways that served me in good fettle throughout the troubles."

"Fascinating," said the Judge; and I could tell by his expression that he was listening with Jed Knickerbocker's ears.

"It is not that I disbelieve you," Mr. Knox interposed. "An old campaigner like yourself must know that frauds abound here. I would hear something in Sioux."

"No offense taken," said Wedlock. Whereupon he paid out a string of guttural intonations of a complex variety that defied question. Even Mr. Knox was impressed. He asked Wedlock what he had said. The saloonkeeper colored slightly.

"Lincoln's address at Gettysburg, or a fair approximation," he confessed. "It was to honor your company and show I've settled that war in my heart."

"Admirable!" exclaimed Judge Blod.

"Did you really meet Chief Red Cloud?" I asked.

"Better than that, lad — Davy, is it? I cured his corns."

"Indians have corns?"

"Bigger than your thumb, every last one of 'em. Comes from climbing over rocks and cactus in moccasins. One of the chief's corns was some older than I was and I soaked it in scalding water and rubbed buffalo grease on it and peeled it off after a week. Injuns never learned about soaking feet. Well, sir, the chief was so happy to have feet like a papoose's he was fixing to adopt me, make me his heir and personal physician. Would of, too, if I didn't see my chance and steal away that very night. I sometimes wonder if I shouldn't of stayed. There's worse ways to live."

"Is that why you wish to serve as our interpreter?" asked Mr. Knox.

"A man can draw a beer just so many ways, sir. He needs to feel a horse between his thighs or he forgets he's a man.

"You know the Black Hills?"

"Better than I wanted to, some days. I scouted them for Custer in '74 and prospected there the next year. I'd likely still be there if I didn't clear out just before the Little Big Horn; picked clean by ants. It was a near enough thing as it was."

"This Ghost Dancing doesn't frighten you?"

He made a motion of dismissal with his mug, which was almost empty now. "Newspaper talk. They've no horses nor weapons. Their warriors are too old and fat to put up a fight and the yonkers are full of mission-school Christ. Half of them don't even speak the lingo. You think old Sitting Bull credits that guff he's spouting about dancing back the buffalo and wearing painted shirts that turn away bullets? He ain't long for this here world himself, so he's stirring them up to die right along with him."

"What luck have you had rounding up volunteers?" the Judge asked.

"Well, it'd be better if you'd say what you want them for. But I'm closing the place at midnight and if you come back then you'll meet what I've got. Mind you, they're friends of old Ben's, and if you don't sign him you'll not find them as willing."

Mr. Knox stiffened. "Blackmail, Mr. Wedlock?"

"I'm just saying they'll do on my word what they wouldn't on a stranger's. Special a stranger that plays his cards as close as you. They've all been snookered before to be what they are, and they didn't none of them forget it."

"It is a prospecting expedition," said Mr. Knox. "Will that satisfy their curiosity — and yours?"

"Them hills was mined out years ago."

"I rather think there is something to be got from them still. In any case that's not your concern. We are hiring an escort, not taking on partners."

"Right enough. They're no hands with picks and shovels." He drained his vessel and rose. "You'll want to talk this out. I'll be at the bar."

When he had withdrawn, Judge Blod glared at me. "There will be no more talk of Quantrill or Flynn. We are assembling an expedition, not a gold rush."

I said nothing, for he was right. My reservations aside, there was something about Ben Wedlock that made me want to confide in him.

Mr. Knox said, "I doubt that fellow has ever seen Virginia, much less lived there.

From his speech he might have left Missouri last week."

"Well, and what of that?" asked the Judge.

"When a Missourian dissembles his origins, it's a fair wager he rode the border. Did you catch that reference to Johnson out front?"

"There were many Johnsons on both sides. It needn't be the one Bloody Bill Anderson defeated after Centralia."

"Even so, I don't believe he ever served with Stonewall Jackson."

"Every other Southerner old enough to have participated in the war claims service with Jackson or Stuart," the Judge said. "If we reject them for that we will be a party of three. We cannot afford to pass up a man who speaks Sioux and knows their habits."

"Perhaps not. We will require a guide with more recent knowledge of the geography."

"Naturally. Meanwhile we require men, and Wedlock has pledged to deliver them."

A muscle worked in Mr. Knox's jaw while he considered. He was thus engaged when the batwings flapped open to admit the man we had seen Wedlock cast out earlier. His overalls were dirtier than before and he had a strawberry streak on one side of his face where he had scraped it when he fell into the street. He was carrying a sawed-off shotgun.

Someone shouted. The shotgun came up and chairs turned over as patrons flung themselves out of the field of fire. Wedlock, standing behind the bar, tugged a short-barreled revolver out of a socket among the beer pulls, aimed along his out-stretched right arm, and shot the man in the chest. The shotgun roared, obliterating most of General Lee's face in the photo-graph over the bar and punching a hole in the ceiling big enough for a boy to crawl through. The man in overalls fell back against the door-frame and slid down, streaking the wood. He finished in a sitting position on the floor with the shotgun be-tween his knees and his chin tucked into his throat.

Silence throbbed. The room was glazed with smoke. It seemed a very long time be-fore someone approached the man on the floor and pried up each of his eyelids. "Deader'n Lincoln."

Only then did Wedlock relax his stance, lowering the pistol. "Fetch the marshal."

The sallow bartender took off his apron and went out the back. Moments later he returned in the company of a small man in a tight black waistcoat and gray pinch hat with a wide flat brim. The newcomer wore gold-rimmed spectacles and black handlebars, and I divined from the brass star in a circle on his waistcoat that this was United States Marshal Julius Honyocker, who had been too busy to attend the inquest on Flynn and Joe Snake. Stepping over the dead man's outstretched legs, he reached down and lifted off the battered hat.

"Anybody know him?" His inflection held a bitter twang.

After a short silence one of the men near the bar spoke up. "Name's Bates, I think. He's got him a little spread out by the canyon."

"Who saw what happened?"

"It was self-defense like I said," announced the bartender. "He did not give Mr. Wedlock no choice."

"Anybody argue with that?"

No one responded.

"Wedlock, I'll use your office for depositions," said the marshal. "If we get enough agreement on the details we'll not need to convene court. I'm closing you down until further notice. This here's the third incident on these premises this year. I warned you last time about your clientele."

Wedlock said, "If he was still clientele he wouldn't of come looking for me with that there splattergun. I run a straight house. You got no call."

"This badge gives me call. Someone push two of these tables together. Two of you men give me a hand with this." Setting aside the dead man's shotgun, the marshal got his hands under the man's arms.

While a temporary bier was thus being assembled, Judge Blod looked to Mr. Knox for a sign.

"He will suffice," said the schoolmaster.

7

Pike's Flight

Marshal Honyocker took our depositions without comment, obtained signatures, and thanked us for our time. Reassured by Wedlock that he would host us later in his padlocked establishment, we returned to the hotel, where the Judge had two bedrooms and a sitting room with a settee sufficient to accommodate a thirteen-year-old boy for the night. With an uncharacteristic flourish, Mr. Knox tossed a blanket roll he had carried from Panhandle onto the settee. "Yours, son," he said. "See to your possibles."

Cautiously — for expansiveness was not his custom — I unbuckled the straps and spread the cover and blanket across the cushions. I then peeled the oilcloth from around two objects calculated to quicken the heart of an adventuresome boy. Jotham

Flynn's Navy Colt's and a Model 1876 Winchester carbine gleamed in the sunlight coming through the windows. I recognized the latter as the weapon Joe Snake had dropped when his horse threw him. Included were two cardboard boxes containing cartridges in .36 caliber for the pistol and .44-40 for the Winchester.

"A man needs protection in sudden country," said Mr. Knox. "There will be time enough to instruct you in their use when we reach Dakota. Mind, you're to shoot only when shot at."

"That is heavy armament for a child," remarked the Judge.

"When I was not much older I could field-dress and reassemble a musket by campfire light. I lied about my age at fifteen in order to join Ledlie's cavalry."

"I was under the impression you were an officer."

"I was promoted from sergeant in the field. Serve your weapons as they serve you, David. They may be your salvation."

"I will. Thank you." It has been my lifelong custom to meet momentous events with reserve.

"No thanks are required. The carbine was Flynn's by right of conquest, the revolver purchased with his money. If he had an heir it is you." He located and opened his satchel, drawing from it a length of parchment that had been rolled into a tube and folded double in packing. "This map of the Black Hills is based on Custer's 1874 survey. I obtained it in Fort Stockton. David, might I borrow Flynn's map?"

I gave him the item, which was always on my person. He unrolled the big map across the cherrywood secretary, weighting down the corners with a lamp and a hand blotter, and spread the Confederate note on top of it. He and the Judge bent over the two illustrations. "No names on these military maps," said Mr. Knox. "This highest peak must be Harney."

They spent most of the afternoon collecting their bearings. At first it was fascinating, but as minutes stretched into hours and the discussion turned from the treasure to equipment and vehicles best suited to the country, it began to sound like one of Mr. Knox's interminable geography lessons. For a time I busied myself with the Colt's and Winchester, learning their mechanisms and admiring their lines and workmanship in a proprietary light. The rail trip and the events of the day — meeting glass-eyed Ben Wedlock, tales of adventure in the war, the killing in the saloon — had exhausted me, and as it was to be a long night I felt that a nap would be wise. I wound the oilcloth around the weapons, rolled them back into the blanket, and made myself comfortable on the settee. Very soon I was dreaming about daring daylight train robberies and bandits' gold.

The dreams became disturbing. In one I clung to a high stone cliff whose nearly smooth features presented few handholds, gazing down at a man climbing toward me in the moonlight. Plainly he was bent upon my destruction. When I attempted to increase the distance between us by ascending farther, I slipped and almost fell. Meanwhile my pursuer was making terrible progress on the slippery rock, hatless and grinning horribly, his angular limbs resembling a spider's. Very soon he was near enough to grasp one of my ankles if he cared. Instead he freed one hand to reach behind his head. Something glinted that turned my bowels to water. . . .

"David! Wake up. It's time."

I lashed out. A lean corded hand caught my wrist. The jolt snapped my eyes open. My first realization was that it had grown dark out. The lamp was burning, casting a globe of buttery light that left the corners black. Mr. Knox's stern face was very close to mine. As he felt me relax, his features softened.

"Nightmares are beneficial to the reasoning process," he said. "They clear out the clabber for the daylight hours. However, I would save my blows for the hostiles."

"Is it midnight?"

"Near enough." He released me and stood back. I rose, quivering a little in my efforts to appear nonchalant. The dream had been vivid.

"Imagination has its place, and this is not it," said another; and now I was aware of Judge Blod standing in the shadows. "Who will keep watch on the trail if one of us must stay up to hold his head?"

"A man without fear is a fool. I fight the war every night in my sleep."

"Just so you have some fight left for the morning."

Amarillo was not safe at night. The railroads delivered as many ruffians as they carried off on their way to and from New Mexico and the Indian Nations, and "knaves and cutthroats," to borrow Jed Knickerbocker's purple phrase, plied the dark streets. A bulge in the right side

88

pocket of Mr. Knox's black frock coat indicated a small pistol, and the way the Judge carried his hickory cane suggested a bludgeon. The staghorn butt of Joe Snake's Schofield revolver protruded through the notch in his waistcoat. I reached for my blanket roll. Mr. Knox stopped me.

"Stay between us. Until I have seen how you shoot, I shall feel safer leaving your arms here."

I wanted to tell him that he could not count upon Judge Blod in the event of a scuffle. I kept silent. The truth seemed a violation of the tenets of partnership.

We reached the Golden Gate without incident. Although the front door was secured with an official-looking iron padlock, a light was burning inside. We followed an alley around behind the building, where the back door admitted us into a combination office and storeroom with a cracked oak desk and crates and barrels stacked to the ceiling. It smelled of tobacco and whiskey.

Through an open doorway and out behind the bar. There stood Ben Wedlock's sallow bartender, gripping the pistol his employer had used that afternoon. Its short barrel was trained on us. Neither the Judge nor Mr. Knox had had the opportunity to produce his own weapon.

"Leather that. You'd be shooting the payroll."

The owner of the familiar voice was seated at a table in the corner by the locked door. Even in repose, Ben Wedlock's solid frame might have belonged to a pine Indian but for his fair hair and face, washed out in the light of a Chesterfield lamp hanging by a chain from the ceiling. The false eye glistened against the patch of burned flesh on his face. Scoured sections of the floor and doorframe marked the scene of the violence earlier.

The bartender let down the hammer and returned the pistol to its socket in the row of beer pulls. I heard another hammer sliding into place, noted Mr. Knox's hand in his right pocket, and realized that he had not been as unprepared as I'd thought. The air cleared.

Wedlock bade us forward. Eight men stood in loose single file in front of the table, attired in everything from distressed buckskins to bowler hats and carrying themselves in that peculiar manner that men have when they are armed. The saloonkeeper himself was using an old Remington revolver to hold down a scrap of coarse brown paper upon which he was scribbling with a gnawed pencil stub no longer than his thumb. The effort of writing was clearly a burden, for he was bent double over the sheet and a pale tip of tongue showed in one corner of his mouth.

"Last name?" he asked.

The first man in line unscrewed the cigar from between his teeth and looked at the end. "Pick one. My paw didn't stay long enough to introduce hisself."

"I got to put something down."

"Hell, Ben, just plain Blackwater's been good enough for you since —"

"Clarence is your Christian, right?"

He chomped down on the cigar. "I don't answer to it."

"Clarence Blackwater then, for the record. Experience?"

"You know all that."

"The record don't."

"I fit with Chivington at Sand Creek and Miles in Montana."

"What else?"

"Let's see, I run a ferry acrost the Muddy by Jeff City till the carpetbaggers shot my pard and taken it over. That was in '68."

"What else?"

"Banking and railroads, I reckon."

The other men in line hooted.

91

"O.K., find a seat. Next."

Blackwater held the spot. "What's the pay?"

"Paymaster's yonder. Ask him."

The recruit came our way. He was tall and built like stretched rawhide, dressed in homespun with a dirty feather in his hatband. His cigar threatened to ignite a set of black whiskers tipped with gray.

"Fifty cents a day," Mr. Knox told him. "Did I hear you say you were at Sand Creek?"

"Wild'n, that was. I bare hung on to my topknot." He scratched his throat.

"I heard it was a massacre of squaws and children."

"Them newspaper writers wasn't there. Fillersteens, Colonel Chivington called 'em."

"What was that remark about banking and railroads?"

"Just a stretcher, Cap'n. The boys liked it."

"Aren't you rather old for this work?"

"Young bucks got too much to lose. I ain't so old in the saddle."

Wedlock was interviewing the next man in line. He was shorter and stouter than his predecessor and had on a stained linen duster and a hat with a rattlesnake band.

He was not much younger than Black-water, although he had a baby face and no whiskers. He was holding a burlap sack at a peculiar angle from his body.

"Christopher Agnes, you still clubbing rattlers for your supper?"

"Not no more. There's better money in bagging 'em live. I know a man in Frisco can't get enough of 'em. Sells 'em to pilgrims for luck. This'n here's worth two bucks if it's worth four bits." He shoved a leather-gloved hand inside the sack and drew out the largest diamondback I had ever seen, holding it behind its ugly squat head while it coiled its body around his arm. Its rattles buzzed. Every man in the room drew back except Wedlock. The baby-faced man cackled.

"Put that up, Christopher Agnes," Wedlock said calmly. "I'm signing men, not sidewinders; though I'm studying on making an exception in your case."

Christopher Agnes pressed a thumb behind the diamondback's head, popping its fangs. A drop of venom plopped to the table. "Old Ike wouldn't hurt *you*, Ben. He'd likely curl up and die."

Wedlock picked up the Remington, cocked it, and aimed it at the reptile's gaping mouth. "He'll do it quicker without brains. You'll just go on like always without yours, but it'll smart. A snake's head makes sorry cover."

Someone coughed in the silence. After a moment Christopher Agnes cackled again and started to return the snake to the sack. Wedlock took the pistol off cock and put it down. Suddenly the diamondback flexed its body, breaking its owner's grip, and sank its fangs into his forearm. He shouted and dropped the snake. In the next instant, half a dozen guns came out. Old Ike's head was obliterated in the fusillade. It thrashed about for almost a minute, then relaxed with a shudder. The room stank of spent powder.

"Someone get a doctor!" cried Mr. Knox.

"No need." Christopher Agnes finished rolling up his sleeve, unfolded a jackknife from his pocket, and slashed the wound in two directions, making a neat X. He sucked out a mouthful of blood and spat it on the floor. Returning the knife, he took a piece of sticking-plaster from another pocket and pressed it to the wound, holding it there until it adhered. "I been bit I bet a hunnert and sevenny-five times," he said. "First ten or twelve I figured I'd kick over sure. Now I just fun a fever. I'll be fit to ride by morning." As he rolled the sleeve back down, I noticed that his arm was mottled all over with X-shaped scars.

Marshal Honyocker came in from the back presently to investigate the shots. Showed the dead snake, he stood sucking a cheek. His spectacles glittered. "Conducting business, Wedlock?"

"This here's a private party," replied the saloonkeeper.

"See it stays private." He withdrew.

After that, the others in line were a blur. Wedlock was interviewing the last man when a newcomer entered. He was slat-thin in clothes that hung on him like wash on a line and his face was a matting of black beard that started just below his eyes and grew down past his chin so that when he grinned, a gold tooth shone like a nugget in a bed of moss. He had a slouch hat pulled low and his right arm hung in a sling of filthy muslin. He was carrying a coiled bullwhip in his left hand.

"Afeared I went and missed it." He squirted tobacco juice into a cuspidor, making it wobble. "Bull's-eye! They ain't ary a soul in Armadillo'd give a honest man the time of night."

His nasal whine had the same effect on me as the shining object in my dream. I grasped Mr. Knox's sleeve. "That is Pike!" I exclaimed, pointing. "The man with the whip the night Flynn was killed!"

Nazarene Pike turned murderous eyes on me. The hand holding the whip drew back. Mr. Knox reached inside his pocket, but before he could bring out the pistol, a metallic crunch announced that Ben Wedlock's reflexes were faster. The Remington was trained on Pike, who froze.

"What's this about killing?" The saloonkeeper's attention remained on Pike, but the question was directed at me.

I glanced at Mr. Knox, who nodded shortly. I said, "He used to ride with Jotham Flynn, the Quantrill man I told you about. He was one of the men who killed him."

"A raider, you say?" Wedlock turned his head my way. Suddenly the whip lashed out, snatching the Remington out of his grasp. Before anyone could react, Pike vaulted the bar and ran out the back. Mr. Knox gave chase, weapon drawn. Presently he returned from the storeroom. "Twice now that man has eluded me," he said. "There will not be a third time. How many other nightriders are you recruiting, Wedlock?"

"None, if I've a voice." Rubbing his

hand, he turned to the bartender. "Hold that man for the marshal if he comes back. Shoot him if he gives you cause. I'll have no bushwhackers on this expedition."

"I think it is up to me what we will and will not have," Mr. Knox reminded him.

"Yes, sir. Just looking out for your interests."

"That fellow seemed to know his way about the place."

"I do a good trade here. I cannot answer for everyone who moves in and out."

The schoolmaster pocketed his pistol. "Wedlock, I've reserved a Pullman and a stock car on the ten-ten to Cheyenne tomorrow morning. You will have your band of heroes at the station. Each man will supply his own provisions and mount, or arrange for them in Cheyenne. This should get them started." He removed a sheaf of notes from his wallet and laid them on the table.

Wedlock seized the money. "Count on us."

"I intend to. What became of the Judge?"

"Present." Judge Blod stepped from behind a coatrack.

As we went out the back, Mr. Knox

asked, "Judge, what have we wrought?"

Behind us, Christopher Agnes was demanding to know who was going to pay him for his damaged rattlesnake.

8

We Begin Our Quest

Our group attracted considerable attention at the depot later that morning. Passengers, greeters, and hangers-on forsook their various pursuits to stare at the men in rough clothes carrying rucksacks and blanket rolls, from the ends of which protruded rifles and carbines of every make and manufacture, yet forswore to ask them what they were about. Those in our party who had horses led them to the stock car for loading and stood around pummeling one another and laughing coarsely at tales of past journeys and adventures. Christopher Agnes arrived with a squirming burlap sack and the notion of hawking live rattlesnakes at every stop; after some persuasion by Mr. Knox and Judge Blod and an exchange of money, he released them in a sandy lot nearby and clubbed them to death with a blackthorn stick he carried for that purpose. The snake-catcher complained of stiffness in the arm that had been bitten ten hours earlier, but otherwise appeared no worse for the experience. Of all my recollections from the time, that one is questioned most often. I have never met anyone else who demonstrated immunity to poisonous snakebites.

And the weapons! Amarillo's ordinance prohibiting the carrying of firearms did not apply to men leaving town, and so the parade of long guns and pistols — thrust inside belts, riding in holsters on hips and under arms, or just simply carried by hand — suggested a convention of gunsmiths. In addition to the expected array of Colts and Winchesters, there were Sharps and Remington buffalo guns, Creedmore competition rifles with mounted scopes, LaMatte .36 caliber pistols equipped with secondary barrels that fired birdshot, pepper-boxes, Greener shotguns. Yellow Boy Henrys, and, in the possession of the man called Blackwater, a British Enfield carbine that he insisted had seen action in the Zulu War of 1879, in the hands of a cousin who had sold his services to Her Majesty's army. In the Texas of 1890, large public displays of percussion weapons were confined to hunting parties and not usually on railroad platforms; hence our celebrity. I confess that I myself carried my blanket roll with the Winchester stock exposed rather higher than necessary.

By contrast with all this ostentation, Ben Wedlock cut a subdued figure in an old Confederate campaign hat with the brim tugged down over his Dresden eye and a canvas coat buttoned over a bulge that I supposed belonged to his Remington revolver. He was carrying a McClellan saddle and pouches and leading a sorrel stallion that stood at least eighteen hands high. True to his prejudice, the animal was all one color. The muscles on its flanks stood out like sculpture. I asked Wedlock what he called it.

"Nicodemus. I've had him ten year come August, and I do believe he's commencing to be a patch on Old Deuteronomy." He laughed when the horse whinnied angrily. "Listen to him. He don't countenance being compared."

"Is that not a Union saddle you have?" I asked.

"I inherited it off a Yankee officer at Second Manassas. I taken the rag for it often enough. If you ride with the stirrups low it's the second next best thing to sitting at home. The *next* best thing is walking." He took his place in line at the bottom of the ramp to the stock car.

"Did you know Robert E. Lee?"

"Seen him horseback once at Sharpsburg. He looked a vengesome angel with his white hair and beard."

"Did you fight for slavery?"

"Didn't none of us do that. Most of us never seen a slave our whole lives, much less owned any. That war wasn't over slavery. We was fighting for Southern independence. You'll hear different, but they're lies."

I changed the subject, for I sensed that I had struck a raw place. "Will we see Indians where we're going?"

"As well ask will we catch fleas in a kennel."

"Are they as savage as Judge Blod says they are in his books?"

"I don't read much. But some are, some ain't, same as white men. One thing you got to have in bushels with an injun is patience. He'll talk about the weather and his wife's piles and how many buffaloes he seen that week and just about anything but the thing you come there to talk about till he runs out of it. Then he'll get to business. But that's talk. If it's your scalp he admires he'll get to it first thing. They got priorities."

"Mr. Wedlock —"

"There ain't been no Mr. Wedlock since a free nigger named Eustace dropped a rooftree on my paw's head accidental-like back in '56," he said. "I'm Ben if you're Davy."

"Ben. Did you know that man Pike?"

"Seen him in there a time or two. I reckon he got wind there was hiring going on. Mind, if I knew he kept company with the likes of Quantrill and Anderson, I'd of run him out before he ever threw a lip over any glass of mine."

"I'm glad. I don't like what I saw of that border trash."

"Someday when you trust me, I'd hear how that came about."

I hesitated. "It is not that I don't trust you."

" 'Course you don't. It's the eye. It was a leg or an arm or even what makes a man a man, you'd call me cripple and pay me what's due. When folks look at me all they see's the eye. You'll get used to it. They all do. I did." His turn came and he mounted the ramp with the sorrel's bit in hand. He handed the reins to a railroad worker sweating in the car and together they struggled against the determined might of the horse, which had set its hoofs and refused to proceed. The railroad man cursed.

"Will I see you in the Pullman?" I called.

"I'd best stay with Nicodemus this trip." Wedlock's voice was strained. "He don't take to travel that ain't his own doing."

Disappointed, I walked down the platform past Marshal Honyocker and two of his deputies, who had evidently been informed that a number of heavily armed men were gathered at the station. The marshal's men were perspiring freely, but in his tight waistcoat and level hat he looked contained in the dry heat. Whatever Mr. Knox and Judge Blod had told him, he seemed satisfied that the situation was moving out of his jurisdiction.

At length the animals were secured, seats taken, and with the conductor's cry of "Board!" the train whistled and slid out of the station. I had a window seat next to Mr. Knox facing Judge Blod, who had begun a log of our journey and was filling pages of foolscap on the tilted surface of an ingenious collapsible writing desk provided by the railroad. His afflicted foot rested in the aisle. I wondered if it would prove a hindrance on the trail.

"Who is meeting us in Cheyenne?" Mr. Knox asked the Judge.

"Major Alonzo Rudeen, the acting commander at Fort Laramie. He has offered us the escort of a patrol as far as the Dakota border. I wrote about him in *Rudeen of Raton Pass*. It played no small role in his promotion."

"Is there anyone out here whom you do not know?"

"We have not met. I based the book upon newspaper reports and information supplied by the War Department. He wrote to thank me. We have been in correspondence since that time."

The tram racketed through countryside that remained constant through that part of the Nations that extends north of Texas, and which has since been renamed the Oklahoma Panhandle; flat yellow earth like crinkled paper, pocked with mesquite and bunch grass, each clump casting a small crescent-shaped shadow looking like the holes that horned toads scoop in the sand just before they vanish beneath the surface. As the day wore on, however, the scenery began to change, subtly at first, then dramatically, becoming green and grassy, the horizon less a straight line as mountains began to take on a deep blue form. I knew

105

then that we were in Colorado. I was now farther from home than I had ever been. Even the air smelled different.

We had an excellent supper in the dining car and retired to our berths for the night. Lying there between the curtains and the curving varnished wall of my wooden womb, I let the car's swaying motion and the mesmeric chattering of the wheels pull me into darkness. This time there were no nightmares, only oblivion.

In Denver the next day, the train stopped for passengers, and we alighted to stretch our legs. I saw Ben Wedlock leading his sorrel down the ramp from the stock car for the same purpose, but as he was deep in conversation with one of the men he had signed in Amarillo, I passed by them after an exchange of greetings. Wedlock seemed refreshed and not at all stiff from what must have been an uncomfortable night in the company of beasts. I saw Christopher Agnes prowling the cinderbed with his stick in one hand and the ubiquitous sack in the other, apparently in vain, for he returned to the Pullman with a dejected aspect.

I was back aboard when a new passenger carrying a worn valise paused just below my open window to ask the conductor if the train was going straight through to Cheyenne. In looks and posture he was ordinary, of middle age and height, with sunburned skin and a brush moustache the color of sand. His store suit and slouch hat were unremarkable and far from new. I could not say what it was about him that interested me. Only when he left the conductor and mounted the next car in line did I place his voice, and even then I was not certain. The West was large, after all. It would contain any number of men whose speech resembled the pleasant tones of Charlie Beacher, one of Nazarene Pike's partners and another of the nightriders who had brought death to my mother's boardinghouse.

9

Philo Hecate

"Judge, I must urge you to reconsider this excursion."

Major Alonzo Rudeen was in his middle thirties and inclined toward stoutness, with a mealy complexion and red muttonchop whiskers that underscored the beginnings of jowls. He wore the full cavalry uniform and gauntlets and a fawn-colored hat with the brim pinned up on one side. His saber slapped his heels as he strode across the Cheyenne platform to shake Judge Blod's hand.

If the Judge found Rudeen's person less heroic than he had imagined, he did not betray disappointment. "Has the situation deteriorated that far?" he asked.

"It has. Moreover, it is still deteriorating. The newspapers have whipped Washington into a fine lather. I expect orders to report with my command to Standing Rock any day. I cannot warrant that you would not be leading your band of civilians into the middle of a war."

"What news of Sitting Bull?"

The major regarded Mr. Knox with a watery stare that he evidently considered martial. "Boiling roots and making dreams in his cabin on Grand River, just as he did at Little Big Horn. Who are you, sir?"

Judge Blod apologized for his poor manners and introduced the schoolmaster and, as an afterthought, myself. I had noticed a distinct drift in his affections away from me since the Joe Snake affair. While he was not precisely hostile, I sensed a distance between us, as between a boy and a man who had no use for him. This sentiment appeared to be shared by Rudeen, who ignored me.

"Young men on the Standing Rock reservation have been observed purchasing arms and ammunition from contraband traders," he said. "Sitting Bull and Wovoka, the Paiute charlatan, have convinced them that if they dance until they drop from exhaustion, the Indian slain will rise, the white man will withdraw from their ancestral lands, and the buffalo will return in numbers. The Sioux believe exclusively that the mystic symbols painted on their shirts will protect them from bullets, which is the most disturbing thing about this entire business, as it means that they are spoiling for a fight. It is a preposterous stew of Christian thought and pagan superstition that can have but one outcome. You would be placing your party in extreme jeopardy if you set out for the Black Hills in this climate."

"Are you ordering us not to proceed?" There was defiance in the Judge's tone.

"I have not that authority. However, I can withdraw my offer of an escort."

"The Rudeen I wrote about was a man of his word."

"I have acknowledged my debt to you, with reservations concerning your more creative flights," said the other. "I am extending this counsel in partial repayment. If you insist upon continuing, I cannot in good conscience refuse protection. I must impose a condition."

"Indeed."

"You know that I may not accompany you into Dakota without orders. This would expose you to the most perilous part of your journey without military protection. I would rest easier knowing you had a guide who is familiar with the country and the current situation. The man I have in mind is a short walk from this place."

"We will welcome the exercise." The Judge caught the attention of Ben Wedlock, who separated himself from the group from Amarillo and came over. "Ben Wedlock, Major Rudeen," said the Judge. "I am placing you in charge until we return. See that no one wanders off."

"Count on me." Wedlock had his good eye cocked toward Rudeen. The major met his gaze with spine straight and chin lifted, and I could feel the barrier between the man in the Confederate hat and the officer wearing the uniform of the Republic.

We took our leave. I paid attention to the people milling around the platform, but did not see the man who had joined us in Denver. He had ridden in a different car, and although I had not seen him alight at any of the stops between, neither had I laid eyes upon him since he came aboard. Assuming that I had made a mistake, I congratulated myself for my decision not to inform Mr. Knox and the Judge of my suspicions. At the time I had been loath to arouse the contempt of Judge Blod — not because I valued his good opinion any longer, but because I valued Mr. Knox's and worried that the other's skepticism might influence it.

Cheyenne had been a cowtown and still smelled like one, but most of the ramshackle saloons and storefronts had given way to brick buildings and, perched on hilltops overlooking the city, ornate houses with turrets and gables and gingerbread porticoes built by railroad men and the wives of cattlemen who spent more time with ledgers than with cows. When our way led toward a saloon of an earlier vintage I supposed that was our destination — Wedlock's Golden Gate and Jed Knickerbocker's accounts having educated me upon the haunts of frontiersmen — but Major Rudeen took us past it and into a frame house down the street. A sign on the porch read HOUSE OF THE BLESSED LAMB.

"Gentlemen," said the major, removing his hat, "allow me to present Deacon Philo Hecate."

It was a long room with a plank floor and two rows of fresh-sawn benches standing on either side of a generous aisle, at the end of which stood a pulpit just as new. Two pointed window openings in each side wall awaited glass. Even as we entered, a man wearing a canvas carpenter's apron planed an eighteen-inch curl off the edge of the pulpit, felt the edge with the heel of a brown hand, and set aside the plane to untie his apron. Beneath it he wore a black cassock and white clerical collar.

He was excessively lean, and would have appeared emaciated but for the strength in his face — clean-shaven, burned dark as ironwood, and made up of flat sections that themselves looked as if they had been planed. His hair was pure white and thick and he had eyes of a disturbing blue clarity, like one of those mountain streams that smoke in the heat of summer and burn one's hands with their iciness. His shoulders were high and thin, his jaw long and square, his mouth a horizontal fissure. When it opened, the words that came out crackled like sticks in a hearth.

"Even Lucifer uncovers in God's house," he said.

Mr. Knox, Judge Blod, and I snatched off our hats. I think we had all forgotten we were wearing them.

" 'And I will raise me up a faithful priest,' " said Deacon Philo Hecate, " 'that shall do according to that which is in mine heart and in my mind: and I will build him a sure house; and he shall walk before mine anointed for ever.' "

"Amen," said the major. "Deacon Hecate hunted and trapped the Black Hills with Carson and Bridger when there were no railroads west of Chicago. He rode with Fremont, established the first mission school in the Dakotas, and until recently ran the mission school at Standing Rock." Rudeen introduced Judge Blod and Mr. Knox. The latter asked Hecate why he left the reservation.

"I could not abide the heathen corruption of the Word."

"May I ask why you wish to return?"

"I did not say that I did."

"The Deacon requires stained glass for his windows," Rudeen explained. "They are costly."

"We are paying a dollar a day for expert services," said Mr. Knox.

"My fee is two dollars a day. I will not work on the Sabbath, and I work only for Christians."

Judge Blod said, "May I inquire as to your age?"

"Three score and eight."

"The excursion will be rigorous enough for a man of thirty," said the Judge. "I cannot foresee a man of near seventy withstanding the hardships."

Deacon Hecate extended his right hand. After a moment, the Judge grasped it. The Deacon squeezed. Judge Blod grimaced and knelt.

" 'And the Spirit of the Lord came mightily upon him,' " said the Deacon, " 'and he rent him as he would have rent a kid, and he had nothing in his hand.' "

Mr. Knox said, "Point taken. If you will release the Judge before his bones are ground to meal, we will meet your price."

He did as requested. Judge Blod rose with Major Rudeen's assistance and stood kneading his hand. Said the Deacon: "I require a Christian band. I do not encourage the company of heathens."

"I cannot promise regular Sunday churchgoers," Mr. Knox replied. "I fancy we are relatively free of Aztecs and Druids."

"Sunday mornings I read Scripture. They may listen or not, each according to the condition of his soul. I will not be interrupted."

"A little Bible-reading would not harm this crew." Mr. Know offered his hand. He was prepared for the clergyman's grip, and I saw surprise and then satisfaction pass across the old man's severe features. When the contest had ended in a draw he asked if we were outfitted.

"That is our next step," said Judge Blod, color returning to his face.

"See Sam Greenspan. His wagons are the stoutest in the territory."

"Greenspan?" Mr. Knox looked amused.

"Christians are more common than good freighters," Hecate confessed. "Tell him you come from me."

Major Rudeen led us down an alley and across a vacant lot to a fenced-in area where a number of Studebaker wagons and one massive and venerable Conestoga stood about in various stages of repair. Half a score of shaggy Percherons grazed inside a corral, the smallest of them twenty hands high with great knobby muscles in its shoulders and thighs. Greenspan, long and thin and bearded and sheathed in gray wool from collar to boots, received us in a combination office and toolroom, heard our needs, perched a pair of black-rimmed pince-nez astride his thick nose to consult a ledger, and said he would have us ready two days hence. Mr. Knox asked him how much money he required.

"Since the Deacon sent you, five hundred dollars."

"How much if he had not?"

"Five hundred dollars. According to him my soul is already forfeit."

Mr. Knox paid him from the fund he

and Judge Blod had created and we went out to arrange lodgings.

"Militarily, spiritually, and personally, we would seem to be fully equipped," said the Judge, after we had parted with Rudeen. "One would think we were starting a colony."

"Not without women," Mr. Knox pointed out.

"Thank the Almighty for that."

I did not take part in this exchange. Since then I have learned the folly of thanking God too soon. But I am getting ahead of myself once again.

10

. . . A Single Step

I shall not burden the reader with the details of our stay in Cheyenne: of how some of us elected to stop at the hotel while others camped out on the prairie and pocketed the sum Mr. Knox had advanced them for rooms for themselves and stabling for their horses, or of the night I accompanied Judge Blod and Mr. Knox upon a visit to the camp and heard the men tell stories around the fire of grisly Indian depredations and sing songs about Dan Tucker, Sweet Betsy from Pike, and a woman named Dora who could do remarkable things with her anatomy. I must, however, share the details of the first meeting between Deacon Philo Hecate and Ben Wedlock, for it had bearing upon what followed.

Wedlock had stabled Nicodemus and

taken a room on the floor below ours. This — surprisingly, in view of the Judge's grumbling about having stood bed and board for men who did not use it — failed to endear him to Judge Blod, who accused the saloonkeeper of pretensions to leadership; although not to his face. Whatever his purpose, we encountered him in the hallway between the shower and his room as the Judge and I were escorting the Deacon downstairs from a conference with Mr. Knox. The Deacon stopped abruptly on the landing. Judge Blod and I had to pull up short behind him to avoid a collision.

"I know you, sir," declared the Deacon.

Wedlock, large and bare-legged in a clean night-shirt strained across his chest and a towel over one shoulder, eyed the clergyman without embarrassment. The saloonkeeper was tidy in his habits, a fact scarcely indicated by the ravaged condition of his face. "You got the advantage, Reverend," he said. "Me and church couldn't make tracks on each other and parted enemies years back."

"Nevertheless we have met. Were you assigned to New York during the late rebellion?"

Something flared quickly and died in the

big man's good eye. It might have been a reflection of the electric light in the hallway. "If you mean the War for Southern Independence, I wasn't. Was you at Second Manassas? If you was, I'd likely know your backside better than your face."

"I served the Union as chaplain. It was the last time I was East." The Deacon appeared unruffled by Wedlock's insinuation. "I feel it is from that epoch that I remember you."

"It's the eye. Last month I shuck loose from this old hag swore I was her son kilt at Shiloh."

"The man I am thinking of was your size, and light of hair and skin."

"You're barking at the wrong old dog, Parson. We never."

The Judge made perfunctory introductions. The Deacon, still chewing over Wedlock's face and figure, said, "You know the Sioux tongue?"

"You don't?"

"I made use of an interpreter at Standing Rock. The hours of the day are few enough to commit the Word to memory without wasting time on archaic languages. You understand the nature of a guide?"

"You point, we head that way."

"With speed. I shall not halt to hunt truants. You will remain at hand in the event of a parley with hostiles. I issue the orders, you follow them. That includes Knox and Blod. Am I clear?" His ice-crystal eyes fixed themselves upon the Judge.

"Reasonably so. The captain of a vessel —"

"Wedlock?"

He showed his fine teeth. "I ain't cut out for command, Padre."

"Deacon."

"Deacon it is. You call the shots with Ben's blessings. This hall's a sight drafty." He nodded at each of us and retired to his room.

"I know that man," Hecate said.

Morning was a steely streak in the east when our party gathered on the flats north of Cheyenne. Sam Greenspan had provided us with three Studebakers with new sheets and rebuilt wheels, each with a team of four: One of these had drawers built into the rear of the box, filled with foodstuffs and cooking utensils, and was placed in the care of Ben Wedlock, who as an innkeeper claimed knowledge of the culinary art; another contained picks and shovels and, for the purposes of our guise as prospectors, an assayer's weigh-scales; the third was empty and would be used to pack the gold back to civilization, although the men were told it was for ore. Mr. Knox and I took charge of the second, and the third was left to Judge Blod, who promptly mounted to the driver's seat and propped his inflamed foot upon the edge of the footboard. He was plainly in discomfort from the dampness of the morning air and, for once, not inclined toward conversation. The men stood about with their horses, stamping their feet in the early cold.

The Deacon had exchanged his cassock and collar for a buffalo jacket with the hide out and wore a stained black hat with a two-inch brim squared over his eyes. Stovepipe boots sheathed his legs to the knees. He approached Mr. Knox and me with a spur-crashing stride that suggested not so much a younger man as an old one who would not slow down for age to catch up. He might have been charging a sinner.

"Where is Rudeen?" he demanded.

"On his way, I should imagine," said Mr. Knox. "Is anything wrong?"

"These men are armed."

"That is the idea. We did not invite them along for their skill at conversation."

"There will be time enough to issue

weapons when we run into trouble. Men traveling long distances scrape up against one another. I would keep altercations at the fistfight level. 'He that smiteth a man, so that he die, shall be surely put to death.' "

"That is not the reason." The schoolteacher raised his chin, taking his eyes out of the shadow of his wide-awake hat.

A muscle worked in the Deacon's jaw. "I've not seen this many cutthroats gathered in one place since Lincoln emptied the prisons to fulfill the 1861 enlistment. Since my back will be to them most of the way, I would draw their claws."

"Why should they mutiny?"

"Because they know as well as I that this is no prospecting expedition."

"And what is it, if not that?"

"You tell me. No man heads into that country at this late date to search for gold not yet dug."

The pair stood silent, facing each other as the sky lightened; the schoolmaster erect and immobile, the preacher-frontiersman swaying as from some awesome dynamo turning deep within his system. Mr. Knox opened his mouth to speak. The measured tread of hoofs interrupted him. Major Rudeen had arrived with his patrol.

Years later, photographs of Colonel Roosevelt attired in full Rough Rider fettle would remind me of the major as he looked that morning, riding a gray gelding at the head of two columns in coat and gauntlets, all personal ungainliness having dropped from him in the act of mounting. The troop's guidons snapped overhead. He called a halt.

"Trouble, Deacon?"

"The holy do not seek it, nor do they shrink from it." The Deacon's gaze was still on Mr. Knox. "I have called for these men to be disarmed."

Mr. Knox said, "They were hired for protection. It makes no sense."

"It does seem a curious request," said Rudeen.

"I do not make requests."

Ben Wedlock joined us. "The men are wondering when we are fixed to move out."

Mr. Knox explained the delay. Wedlock listened, took off his hat, scratched his fair head, and covered it. After a moment he reached under his coat and brought out the Remington. The major's hand twitched toward his holster flap. Wedlock spun the pistol then and offered it to the Deacon, butt foremost.

"Honest folks don't need iron when things are quiet," he said.

The Deacon accepted the weapon and handed it without looking to a man near him. This was a pale scarecrow half the Deacon's age in a Mormon hat and chesterfield. In the poor light I had thought him to be another of the Cheyenne volunteers, but I saw now that he was of a different stripe.

"This is Elder Sampson," said the Deacon, as if the question had been spoken aloud. "He travels with me. Put it in the empty wagon," he directed. "Place all the weapons there."

The man called Sampson moved off to obey. Wedlock started after him. "I'll see to it."

"*I* shall see to it. You are the organizers," the Deacon told Mr. Knox and the Judge, who was listening from the wagon, "but this expedition is mine. We shall talk further." He strode away briskly.

"That man has his eye on the Throne of Heaven," remarked the Judge darkly.

"He tends to seize the reins," Rudeen said. "What counts is he will bring some of you through alive."

"I like him." Mr. Knox turned to Wedlock. "You'd best keep him company. Brave

125

men are fools oftener than cowards; and even honest men resent sermons so early on a working day."

"They are spirited," agreed the saloonkeeper, taking his leave.

To me Mr. Knox said, "Fetch your carbine and pistol, David. If we are to lead, it must be by example."

"It does not seem to me that we are leading at all," I said. He made no reply.

It may have been the Deacon's stern demeanor, or more likely it was the presence behind him of Ben Wedlock, but little more than grumbling accompanied the call for the surrender of weapons. Swiftly the bed of the wagon filled with all manner of devices, from ancient cap-and-balls to scoped target rifles still gleaming with factory oil. Bowies, stilettoes, daggers, skinners, scalpers, and "Arkansas toothpicks" joined the pile, glittering like fangs. I contributed my firearms and Mr. Knox added a fine nickel-plated Colt's Lightning and an 1873 Winchester. Judge Blod handed me Joe Snake's notched Schofield to place on the stack, which Elder Sampson rearranged to avoid nicks and scrapes and covered with a canvas tarpaulin. I noticed that he smelled strongly of lavender water.

"That's the kit," announced Wedlock finally.

"Except for the hideouts," Deacon Hecate said. "We shall gather those as they surface."

At last the wagons were drawn into line: Mr. Knox's first, followed by Ben Wedlock's and then the one containing the weapons with Judge Blod at the reins. The cavalry took its position in front with the Deacon sitting a great bony claybank beside Rudeen's gray and Elder Sampson straddling a bay mule behind the wagon containing the weapons. The Amarillo volunteers formed a snaggled formation at the rear. I had been assigned to ride with Mr. Knox, but begged his leave to join Ben Wedlock aboard the chuck wagon. The schoolmaster regarded me from the driver's seat.

"Smitten, are you?"

"He does not address me as a child," I said.

"You are not a man."

"I do not need reminding."

"Be wary, David. Men are seldom as they seem, and those that are may be the most dangerous of all."

"Am I forbidden?"

"Would your mother forbid you?"

I hesitated. "I think she would not."

"I think she would." He squinted into the rising sun. "However, I am not your mother."

"I may go?"

"Hadn't you better ask if you are welcome?"

I thanked him and did just that at the next wagon in line. Wedlock grinned, winked his good eye, and tossed a coil of rope and some other truck into the bed to make room for me on the seat.

There wasn't time for talk. Leaving Rudeen, the Deacon cantered to a rise, wheeled to face the party, and removed his hat. The sun came up red behind him. The wind stirred his hair, white as birch ashes.

" 'We have dealt very corruptly against thee,' " he began, in a voice that was not loud, but whose resonance swept like summer thunder over the flats, " 'and have not kept the commandments, nor the statutes, nor the judgments, which thou commandest thy servant Moses.

" 'Remember, I beseech thee, the word that thou commandest thy servant Moses, saying, if you transgress, I will scatter you abroad among the nations;

" 'But if ye turn unto me, and keep my

commandments, and do them; though there were of you cast out unto the uttermost part of the heaven, yet will I gather them thence, and will bring them unto the place that I have chosen to set my name there.

" 'Now these are thy servants and thy people, whom thou hast redeemed by thy great power, and by thy strong hand.

" 'O Lord, I beseech thee, let now thine ear be attentive to the prayer of thy servant, and to the prayer of thy servants, who desire to fear thy name; and prosper, I pray thee, they servant this day, and grant him mercy.' "

"Amen," he finished, and for the space of ten seconds there was silence except for the wind threading the grass, and behind us the inveterate splattering of tobacco juice from among the Amarillo irregulars. Then Hecate put his hat back on, stood in his saddle, and swept his long right arm forward. The procession started unevenly, like a chain tautening: first the Deacon, then Rudeen's cavalry, then Mr. Knox's wagon. Ben Wedlock picked up his reins.

"A thousand-mile journey begins with a single step, Davy," said he, flipping them. "Chief Red Cloud told me that himself."

And as we started with a lurch, he broke
into a song that was seized and borne
along by the men at the rear:

Oh, I'm a good old rebel,
now that's just what I am!

11

The Blaze-Face Horse

Oh, it was a grand adventure!

I have done many things in a life that I may with some modesty consider to have been eventful, and met men enough to fill any body of memoirs, but for richness and excitement the intervening years have yielded no crop to match that early harvest.

The reader has already met Blackwater, who fought with John Chivington of evil memory and told stories of Nelson Miles's thirteen-hundred-mile pursuit of Chief Joseph and the Nez Perce to the border of Canada; and Christopher Agnes, whom I saw catch a grandfather diamondback in mid-strike in his bare hands and, in almost the same motion, whirl it around by its tail and dash out its brains against the trunk of a cottonwood, then curse the reflexes that had cost him such a fine specimen. Add to them a Negro wrangler named Eli Freedman with a withered arm he claimed to have burned when General Sherman set Atlanta to the torch, and who seemed far more at ease with the horses in his charge than with his fellow men; a long-haired dandy named Mike McPhee, who had toured with Colonel Cody's show until the Colonel fired him for paying attention to a trick rider the Colonel admired himself, and boasted, in an Irish brogue as thick as turned earth, that he could pluck out a prairie dog's eye at forty paces with either hand, had he but access to the matched and specially balanced Americans that now resided in the wagon with the other weapons; and Bald Jim, whose surname was never known to me, whose benign aspect and prematurely nude scalp moved the younger members of the party to call him Dad, and who, Wedlock confided, had slain three Arapaho braves who broke into his cabin on the Powder River during the terrible winter of 1873, then eaten them. Any one of them had seen and done more than the five younger men that Mr. Knox had recruited in Cheyenne put together.

And of course there was Ben Wedlock

himself, he of the quiet speech and terrible countenance, who served as trail cook and was never heard to issue an order, but who moved among the civilian volunteers with an air of command unchallenged. For all that he stressed a sedentary attitude, affecting discomfort with the chuck wagon's bumpy motion and an old man's groan of relief when at the end of the day he lowered himself to the ground with the others around the fire. I, who had seen him leap into his seat of a morning like a boy one third his age, and who had hung on while he whipped the team forward to keep the road when a wheel dropped into a hole that would have upset a lesser man's wagon, was not taken in by this artifice, although others were. It is a curious habit of some older men to exaggerate their infirmities.

From the start, however, I was in his trust. Sometimes during the day he would pass the reins to me, sit back, charge a blackened lump of pipe, and tell of the bad times while mountains rolled past under tall sky.

"The chief had a niece he was fixed to marry onto me," he said one afternoon. "Her name was Spring Shower or somesuch; they don't always translate, injun names. Anyway she was pretty as they go, but you got to look at the older squaws to know how they'll wind up. Well, I got out before anything come of it. I don't know, though. There's lots worse ways to live. Lots worse."

"How did you escape?"

"My guard went to sleep. Guard duty bores an injun. I parted his hair with a rock just to make sure and cut out one of the chief's horses. I seen Red Cloud at the agency years later, after the peace. He didn't hold it against me about his niece nor the brave I split open; but he did want to know what become of the horse."

"Did you ever marry?"

"Married a storekeeper's daughter in Council Bluffs. They was the only fambly for miles wasn't Mormon. It didn't take. I moved flour sacks and sold sardines for a year and left when snow was on the ground. I never looked back on it. I guess the old man's dead by now. I'd be a storekeeper with ten kids. But I never could make tracks on them Mormons."

Judge Blod suffered mightily with his gout and took to the back of his wagon nights, where he had cleared a space among the confiscated weapons and lay moaning with his foot propped on a stack of revolvers. One night Ben Wedlock persuaded him to let him wrap the foot in a poultice he had made from sage and cottonwood bark and rock mold, dried and then boiled and wrapped in damp ticking. The Judge was instructed to keep it on when he slept and to leave his boot off in the morning. The procedure was repeated the next two nights, at the end of which the Judge began to feel better, and by the time we drew within sight of South Dakota, his pain had ceased. His earlier reservations about the one-eyed man's character forgotten, he pronounced Wedlock a wizard and proposed to write a book about his past adventures to show gratitude. Genially Wedlock declined. When we were alone I asked him if the poultice was an Indian remedy.

"Made it up on the spot," he said with a wink. "Tell a man you'll cure what ails him and if he's in enough misery he'll cure himself."

The Bad Lands had intrigued me since I first heard the name. Encountered at first hand, the country was planed flat by wind and glaciers and cluttered, as by a great diffident hand, with granite towers and sandstone cliffs butting into blue sky, their surfaces tapped and fluted like refugee parts from a machine shop. This was the Red Valley, scarped incongruously with gray Dakota sandstone fanning out from a charcoal-colored blister that Ben Wedlock informed me constituted the storied Black Hills. There for the first time I understood the Indians' insistence that the region was sacred. How to explain those jarring features, if they were not placed there as part of some divine perverted plan? The wind razored their square edges with a half-human chant.

"This is good-bye," said Major Rudeen one dawn, when the shadows of the buttes and needles clawed the ground. He had ridden out to reach down and shake the Judge's hand from his seat aboard the gray. "Any farther and I will be in violation of the treaty. Again I must implore you to abandon this quest."

"Thank you, Major. The thing is in motion." Judge Blod's mood was jovial. His foot was booted once more and planted in a normal position on the board.

"It would grieve me to see that fine white scalp decorating some buck's lodgepole."

"No more than it would me, I assure you. The Deacon will see us through."

136

The patrol left us in column-of-twos, pulling a shadow as long as the major's face as we last saw it. Shivering a little — the morning air was brisk — I took my leave of the Judge and mounted the seat beside Wedlock. He was staring at the hills.

"I never lay eyes on them without my gut draws up," he said. "More hair's been lifted over them than flies in a pasture."

"Are Indians as bad as everyone says?"

"No good nor bad to it out here, Davy. Just dying and living and trying to do the one without the other." He drew into line behind Mr. Knox's wagon and tied off to wait. The air still smelled of woodsmoke and grease from breakfast.

"Judge Blod calls them savages in his books. But I guess you don't have to be an Indian to be a savage."

"You're wise beyond your years, Davy. I've ridden with men twice your age didn't have half your brains."

I glowed at these words. "What makes a man come to this country, Ben?"

"Depends on the man. Some come running ahead of the law. Some pack it in with them. Some bring God, like the Deacon there. I reckon the rest just come looking for a place to be born all over again."

"Why did you come?"

He smoked his pipe. "Well, Davy, I done my share of running, no use denying it. I was a wild'un when I was a yonker, though I don't reckon there's innocent blood on these hands. I wore a star myself a time or two, if you can feature it. Everyplace I went, God was there first if you looked for him. The getting born all over, now; that never lost its shine. There ain't that many places left a man can do that. I'll miss it when it's gone."

Just then the procession started, crossing the invisible line into the country of the Sioux — and of Quantrill's buried gold. He untied the reins and took them between his fingers. "Yes, sir," said he, releasing the brake, "I'll sure miss it."

Coming up on midday we saw our first Indian. He appeared atop a rise as suddenly as if he had been conjured, seated astride a whitestocking black with nothing but sky behind him and only his long hair stirring in the wind to indicate that he was anything but carved out of the hill. In leggings and breechclout and blue cavalry coat and campaign hat he was like a spirit caught between worlds, with a carbine slung from a strap over his shoulder, quiver fashion, and his feet in moccasins and the moccasins thrust into conventional white man's stirrups. Ben Wedlock, following the wagon ahead, sensed my excitement.

"Easy down, Davy. He don't mean us no harm."

"How can you tell?"

"Because we can see him."

And then, as quickly as he had appeared, he was gone. After a moment he came around the curve of the hill farther down, leaning inside, back arched and one arm hanging as if coming in at an easy lope, although the black was in full gallop. Queen Victoria on her seventieth birthday could not have shown more grace.

Deacon Hecate, sitting his bony claybank at the head of the column, raised a hand and the visitor drew rein thirty yards short and again sat motionless, his black shaking its head and throwing lather. Presently the Deacon turned in his saddle and caught Wedlock's eye. Wedlock pulled the chuck wagon out of line and we joined our guide.

"A Sioux policeman out of Standing Rock," Hecate reported. "I know him not, but that's a grain-fed mount he is riding, with an army brand."

"He's a deal from home," said Wedlock.

Mr. Knox pulled his wagon abreast of

ours. "What business has he here?"

"One way to find out." Wedlock made a sign. After a pause the Indian signed back. His movements were as graceful and economical as his horsemanship. "He wants a parley."

"Tell him to come in," said Hecate.

The black picked its way through the fallen rocks at the base of the hill. Up close the Indian was young, not more than ten years older than I, his face made up of ovals, with a thick nose and dark eyes from which the lashes had been plucked. He was naked-chested under the army coat and wore a Colt pistol with a smooth cedar grip in a holster on his right hip. He said something in a harsh guttural.

"He wants to know who we are and why we're here."

"Ask him the same thing."

The Indian appeared to think it out. Finally he replied at length.

"You was right about Standing Rock," Wedlock told Hecate. "This here is Panther, a corporal with the Indian police there. He's tracking a band of renegades bolted the reservation ten suns back. Their leader calls himself Lives Again and he's got him a bellyful of the Ghost Dance sickness. That's what Panther calls it anyway."

"He's tracking them alone?"

Responding, the Indian pulled open the right side of his coat, where a raw scar bisected his rib cage. It had bled recently and dried yellow-brown.

"He says five of them was ambushed by Lives Again's men hiding in the rocks. The others was kilt. He played possum and got two of Lives Again's bunch when they came down to finish him off. The others ran."

"Why has he not gone for help?"

When Panther spoke this time, I saw that he was not young at all, whatever his years were. There was a deadness in his eyes, and a setness to his cracked lips that might have been described, on a white man, as a grim smile.

"He says that he has sung his song and that it's a good day to die."

"Heathen," muttered Hecate; but it was plain from his tone that he was not unmoved. "Ask him where he thinks this Lives Again is now."

"I know English."

We stared, as if at a graven head from which words had issued. The Deacon broke the silence. "Why did you not say so before?"

"When dealing with strange white men I

prefer time to choose my words." Panther spoke carefully, as one who is not thinking in the language in which he is speaking. "You come to this place with many questions but no answers."

"We are prospectors," said Mr. Knox. "I am Henry Knox. These gentlemen are Philo Hecate and Ben Wedlock. The boy is David Grayle."

The Indian regarded me. "He is old enough for manhood." To Wedlock: "Go back, False Eye, or leave your bones. The gold is gone from this place."

"Are you threatening us?" Hecate pointed his chin. " 'Am I a dog, that thou comest to me with staves?' "

Now the expression on Panther's lips was a smile indeed, albeit a sad one. "The words of Goliath. The Philistine. I am the son of Gray Fox, who laid your fire winter mornings. You grow old, Deacon, that you forget those whom you taught your Bible."

Hecate seemed only slightly taken aback by this revelation. "Not well, or you would not speak of it as mine."

" 'Thy belly is like a heap of wheat.' " He was still smiling. "My wife's is the color of clay. I think that it does not speak to us."

"Where is Lives Again?" demanded the Deacon a second time.

"Not far. I found a pile of manure with the steam rising from it this morning. He has twenty braves with him. They have sworn to murder every white man they find in the Black Hills. It is not my business. My business is to die. I have sung my song." He gathered his reins. "You would do well to sing yours, or else leave this place." And before any of us could address him again, he spun and galloped back the way he had come. The hill swallowed horse and rider.

"They will not all come to Jesus," said the Deacon sadly. "Get back into line."

"Should we arm the men?" Mr. Knox asked.

"There will be time for that. If young Panther has not just been smoking up dreams."

"What did he mean about singing?" I asked Wedlock, when the formation was regained.

"His Death Song." The saloonkeeper knocked out his pipe and put it away in his clothes. "When an injun gets ready to die he sings to the Great Spirit for courage and goes out."

"To die?"

"Be kind of foolish to sing the Death Song and then go out for a beer."

"Will Panther die?"

"If he goes up against twenty renegades I don't see he's got a choice."

"That is the most heroic thing I have ever heard."

"That's the idea."

"Ben?"

He grunted.

"Would you ever do it?"

"I already did once."

He involved himself with the traces then, putting an end to the conversation. But I was burning to know the story.

We saw no more Indians nor anyone else that day. At evening, Mr. Knox, Judge Blod, and the Deacon gathered at the rear of Mr. Knox's wagon to discuss the route through the Black Hills. Bored by this geography lesson, I set out to find Wedlock, who was relaxing after supper with the Amarillo party. Mr. Knox called me back.

"David, see to Cassiopeia, will you?" He had brought the mare from home to serve as a saddle horse.

"That is Eli Freedman's duty," I pointed out.

"She is off her feed. I don't trust him to keep after her until she eats."

"Can it wait until later? I was going —"

"I would deem it a favor."

I could not refuse, although I knew the request was but a design to prevent me from spending more time with Ben Wedlock than Mr. Knox considered necessary. Ruminating upon the difficulty with which old conflicts died, I took myself under a naked three-quarter moon to the ridge where the horses were picketed. The Black Hills loomed darker than night beyond: ancient, feral, sinister in their crouched attitude.

Eli Freedman was absent — availing himself, I supposed, of a late supper now that the mounts were fed and made ready for the night. He seldom dined with the others. I had been told that this was his way going back to the time he was burned trying to rescue plantation horses from a blazing stable during the siege of Atlanta. Thus unobserved, I determined that Cassiopeia was indeed content, and turned to leave. Something white caught my eye.

At first I thought it was a patch of moonlight on the forehead of Wedlock's sorrel Nicodemus, but upon investigating I found that it was fixed in place. I had not noticed it in all the time the horse was tied to the back of the chuck wagon during our trek through Wyoming. Suspecting a bird passing overhead, I licked my thumb and

rubbed at the spot. Nicodemus flinched —
as did I, for the thumb came away streaked
not with white, but with the reddish brown
of the stallion's coat.

Curious, I plucked a handful of grass
damp with evening dew and scrubbed at
the animal's forehead, clutching its mane
to prevent it from shying. Slowly the dark
color came off. I stepped back, dropping
the stained grass. A chill gnawed at my vi-
tals. Before me was the blaze-face horse
belonging to the one-eyed man who had
superintended the murder of Jotham
Flynn.

12

What I Heard

I had scarcely time to digest this revelation when the sound of approaching voices alerted me to my own danger. To be discovered staring at the awful evidence would have been fatal; for among those voices I heard the bantering, storytelling tones of Ben Wedlock. Without thinking I scrambled down the other side of the ridge. In the shadow of the hill my foot found the burrow of some small animal and I fell headlong into the tall grass, emptying my lungs and stunning myself momentarily. The horses, unsettled by so much unexplained movement, stamped and snorted and tugged at their pickets.

"Here, what's with the horses?" I recognized Mike McPhee's brogue.

"Eyes open," Wedlock admonished.

"Horses draw injuns like gnats."

Yellow light came over the ridge in a counterfeit dawn. Flattening myself further — I was stretched out on my stomach now — I saw the Irishman's profile on the crest with lantern raised. He passed it around in a wide arc, startling the horses into fresh transports. I buried my face and felt the light sliding over my back. Finally he lowered it. "Nothing."

"Varmint." The single word belonged to Christopher Agnes. "They're what snakes was invented for."

"Go on, Black Ben. You was at St. Louis."

"Mind that!" snapped McPhee.

"Aw, that Bible-banging old bastard won't hear us up here." I could not place this voice, and decided it belonged to one of the young men who had joined us in Cheyenne.

Wedlock said, "Just the same, call me Ben. Well, St. Louis. We dropped a tree across the tracks and when she stopped, Pike and me boarded and throwed down on the engineer and brakeman. Beacher was riding the cars and had the conductor pinned back by that time. Then Bloody Bill come up with Flynn and the rest. The eye was my doing. When the shooting commenced I lost concentration and that engineer jerked this old knuckle-duster out of his back pocket and let fly at my face. It was the powder flash done it; the ball had fell out if it was ever in or I wouldn't be here jabbering. I reckon I done for that engineer while I was still howling.

"I wasn't good for much after that, though I got mounted and made it to our first camp. It was Bloody Bill told me he couldn't stop to see I was took care of; said Shelby'd be along directly and his sawbones'd fix me up proper. Well, we both knowed he was lying in his whiskers, but I reckon I looked not long for this here world or he'd of put a ball through my other eye to keep me from talking to the bluebellies."

"What happened?"

I was struck by the thought that the young man from Cheyenne sounded much like me.

Christopher Agnes said, "He died."

"Stop funning the boy. It was the Yanks found me. Told 'em I was with Shelby or they'd of hung me on the spot to save powder. I was halfway to Elmira with a patch on my eye by the time they worked it out, if they ever did."

"You spent the rest of the war in prison?"

"Busted out when I was up for it and hiked back. Took me six months. By the time I caught up with Pike and Beacher and the rest Bloody Bill was dead. Flynn had lit out and it wasn't till the shooting stopped on both sides we put together what became of the gold. When that paymaster Peckler turned up dead in Amarillo and Flynn got sent to Huntsville we knowed for sure. That's when I set up shop in Amarillo; if there was a way to that gold, there's where it'd start. Mind, if I knowed it'd take twenty years I'd of found a better one. Ah, but then I would never of hitched up with you, Tom. You're wise beyond your years and hang the rat that says different. I've ridden with men twice your age didn't have half your brains."

I felt ill to hear him plying another young man with these familiar words. However, I had not the opportunity for self-pity because of the turn the conversation took at that point.

"Who's with us?" Wedlock inquired.

"Just Tom here in that Cheyenne crowd," said McPhee. "They're older and the straight wages look sweet to them. But Blackwater's adjusting their case. We might be obliged to help one or two along to

150

judgment and then the rest will see their way clear enough."

Wedlock said, "The Deacon's lost to us for sure. Every time I lay eyes on him I see him walking the row at Elmira sticking Jesus through the bars. What about Sampson?"

McPhee made a noise of Celtic contempt. "When Hecate buys the farm, expect the Elder to wait by the rock three days. He don't wring out his own mop but that the Deacon gives him leave."

"He sleeps under that wagon," Christopher Agnes added. "Blod sleeps harder than harsh justice inside but there's no getting the guns without stirring up Elder Sampson."

"There's hazards out here. That jackass of his could put her foot wrong any day and pitch him headwise into a rock."

Wedlock delivered this pronouncement over a yawn. I felt a chill that had little to do with the damp grass upon which I lay.

"Where's Pike and Beacher?" McPhee asked. "I calculated they'd be here before this."

"Trailing, like I told them." The saloonkeeper yawned again. "We're laying ruts a Yankee clerk could follow. They'll be here come the time. Don't waste your water worrying over it till then."

"When *is* the time?"

"Possess your soul in patience, Tom. Let Knox and Blod find the gold first. There's no sense in us doing the work, with them so eager."

"What then?"

Christopher Agnes cackled. "I get the Deacon. Let me punch in his skull with my stick and you can split the schoolteacher and Judge Moldy Toe 'twixt you."

"The boy too?" asked Tom.

"Leave the boy to me," Wedlock said.

"Ben, look here."

Something in McPhee's tone, coming on top of the other's ominous statement, made me shrink closer to the earth. Figures moved in the lantern light at the top of the ridge. I smelled Wedlock's pipe.

He cursed. "Red Hannah swore to me the stuff would hold in a Missouri rainstorm. Tom, go down and fetch me that black pot from my wagon, the one with the cover."

Footsteps retreated in the direction of camp.

"Someone's wiped it off deliberate," McPhee said. "Where's the nigger?"

They had discovered the sorrel's exposed blaze. My heart began to bang.

"Down having his supper. He didn't do it." Wedlock sounded thoughtful. "It sweated off. We'll have to watch for that. Damn Hannah."

"It couldn't all sweat off."

"Know the stuff, do you?"

McPhee did not respond. "If you changed horses we wouldn't be worrying over it."

"You'd not say that if you saw Nicodemus on the flat. I'm standing here now on account of he won't be beat. And the boy saw the blaze the night Flynn bought the farm."

"You might could sell the boy a piece of it," Christopher Agnes suggested.

"We kill him now we tip our hand. Besides, they've all seen the horse without a blaze. We'll just have to watch for it like I said."

"I say someone wiped it off." McPhee took two steps down my side of the ridge and lifted the lantern. The light swung my way.

"Lower that," Wedlock said. "You want the whole camp up here?"

The edge of the light touched my hand, wavered. I was tensed to spring up and flee.

"Is this what you wanted?" It was Tom's

voice. "There's the boy," Wedlock said. "Hang on to it while I smear it on. Mike, the light."

The light was withdrawn. My hand felt cooler. No one spoke after that, although I heard Ben Wedlock humming "I'm a Good Old Rebel" as he covered the blaze with red hair dye. I took advantage of their concentration to crawl backward to the bottom of the ridge. There I rose in darkness and started off around to where I had left Mr. Knox and the others. I was shivering with shame and betrayal.

13

We Draft a Plan

"I *knew* it, under God!"

As he said this, Deacon Hecate smacked his left palm with his right fist, producing a sound not unlike a crack of wrathful thunder. "Did I not say I remembered him from New York? That face stood out even among Elmira's Godless!"

Judge Blod, looking repentant, had joined the group at Mr. Knox's wagon. "I must assume responsibility. It was I who found Wedlock and pressed for his inclusion. I above all should recognize a desperado when I see one."

"We were all fooled. And I rather think it was Wedlock who found you. He is cleverer than he appears." Mr. Knox was calculating. "He has managed to stack this expedition with his fellow guerrillas and to seduce one of the Deacon's volunteers under our very noses. It is no wonder that Bloody Bill found him indispensable."

"Thief and murderer," said the Judge. "And very near Mephistopheles to Master Grayle's Faust."

"More accurately, the swan to David's Leda. I think that even the Deacon will agree that David's soul is firmly in his body's keeping."

"He was my friend, I thought." It shames me to relate that I was very near to tears.

Mr. Knox laid a hand upon my shoulder. "You have had a hard lesson. Some men will assume any guise in order to fulfill their greed."

"Now you will tell me what we are about." The Deacon's graven countenance belonged to a vengeful angel. "Killers and brigands do not plot for honest gold."

"There is little point in maintaining the secret." Judge Blod told him of the train robbery, of Flynn's death, and of the Yankee bullion hidden in the Black Hills. For illustration he bade me produce the map. The Deacon glowered over it.

"I shall keep this. It is all that stands between us and the fate these cutthroats have in store for the honest men of this expedition."

Mr. Knox said, "It is better left with David. Wedlock would not expect it to be in a mere boy's possession."

After a moment, the Deacon returned it to me. "A child shall lead them."

"We cannot turn back without forcing a fight. Meanwhile we remain in their clutches," said the Judge. "One of us must ride back and fetch Rudeen's column."

"I will!" I was eager to redeem myself.

"He said that we were on our own when he left us," Mr. Knox reminded him. "You know the man. Would he disobey orders to help a friend?"

"No." The Judge was solemn. "He is too much the good soldier for that. However, in the absence of alternatives it seems worth the attempt."

Mr. Knox shook his head. "It would leave us short a man — or a boy. Whoever we sent, the guerrillas would be bound to notice his absence and start the show."

"So much the better. If we send the boy, we will still be eight and they are seven. And we have access to the weapons."

"You forget Pike and Beacher, who will certainly come up to join their confederates at the sound of a battle. We cannot assume the cooperation of the four men from Cheyenne whom Wedlock has not reached, after having kept them in the dark so long about the nature of this excursion. For which I accept my share of the blame," Mr. Knox added. "Also, the Deacon has already postulated the existence of hideout guns among the party.

"We are in a fair fix." Judge Blod looked old and frail.

The schoolmaster did not. "We have not considered the obvious."

"No!" barked Deacon Hecate, whose brain was working faster than either the Judge's or mine.

"Hear me out. If gold can buy the support of the men from Cheyenne for the guerrillas, it can as well buy it for us. But we must work fast. Many a war has been decided by such businesslike methods."

"And many a soul lost." In his righteous wrath, the Deacon appeared younger — yet far older; as old as the bedrock upon which the Black Hills stood — than Judge Blod. "I shall not proposition loyalty."

"Wedlock will if we do not, depend upon it. His kind is not bound by laws or Scripture."

"The Apocalypse is upon us," snarled the other. Plainly, he had surrendered the point.

"Wedlock's delay has given us grace."

Mr. Knox did not pause to mourn the demise of the Deacon's principles. He again grasped my shoulder. "David, I have a difficult chore for you. It will be harder than anything you have ever attempted."

"Worse than geography?"

He did not laugh. "I want you to return to Wedlock's side and behave as if you still thought you were friends."

"Is this wise?" asked the Judge.

"It is more than wise. It is unavoidable."

"I don't wish to see him ever again," I said.

"That is the difficulty. We require this time to canvass the Cheyenne volunteers for their support in the coming fight. You have already saved our lives by overhearing Wedlock's intentions. I must now ask you to go back and keep your ears and your eyes open and report to me what you have heard and seen. David, you are our one hope."

"I will do it!"

"There's a lad! Deacon, the Judge and I must request the return of our handguns. You will be prudent to arm yourself as well."

Soberly the man of God unfastened his buffalo coat and opened it to reveal the yellow bone handle of a pistol concealed in one hairy inside pocket. " 'And his sling was in his hand,' " he said.

"I shall need my Navy Colt's," said I.

Mr. Knox said, "In time you shall. For now it would be more dangerous for you to go armed. Everything must appear as normal."

We repaired to the wagon where the weapons were stored. There I stood watch while the Deacon explained the situation to Elder Sampson, who listened without comment and then allowed Mr. Knox and Judge Blod to reclaim their pistols. The Deacon then cautioned Sampson about the plot to murder him and make it appear an accident.

"It will be — for them." It is the only one of the Elder's rare remarks I remember in detail.

Presently I saw the lantern descending the ridge where the horses were picketed, and announced this to the others, who concealed weapons and tied down the wagon flap. "Remember, David," said Mr. Knox; "everything as before. We are counting on you."

And so I set out to play my role. I did not overlook the disturbing fact that the last time I had heard these parting words, they had been told me by Jotham Flynn on the morning of the last day of his life.

14

The First Shot

Little conversation passed between Ben Wedlock and myself upon his return from the ridge. This was mostly my doing, for despite the responsibility I had been given, I could not be garrulous that night. Hours after the camp bedded down I lay awake in my blanket beneath the chuck wagon. Wedlock breathed evenly nearby, and the moonlight glittering off his glass eye between lids that never quite closed was no aid to rest. Supine, he loomed very large, the ogre of all my nightmares.

Most of them, in any case. When I finally surrendered consciousness, I found myself clinging, as in my dark Amarillo dream, to a rocky cliff many leagues high. Below me my pursuer inched closer with each breath, a terrible tobacco-stained grin

161

smearing his black-bearded face when I lost my footing and nearly pitched into his arms. As I caught myself, a shaft of light found his narrow rodent's features and gold front tooth. They belonged to Nazarene Pike, he of the coiled bullwhip and fleetness of foot when I denounced him in the Golden Gate Saloon as one of Jotham Flynn's murderers. Again I reached the end of my climb and could go no farther; again I saw his hand dart behind his head, the shining something come out. I awoke with a cry.

In a trice Wedlock was upon me, one trunklike arm braced behind my neck and the other across my face, the hand gripping the side of my head. His big face with its blackened left side and dead eye was terrifyingly close. (How could I not know that countenance as the one Flynn had described to me with such fear and loathing?) A single twist and my neck would be broken.

Recognition seeped slowly into his fierce expression. He relaxed his grip. I resumed breathing.

"I near done for you that time, Davy," he said, and — oh, dissembling villain! — his voice shook. "You must never spook old Ben. I kilt a Cheyenne breed on the Rocky

Ford that same way in '78."

"Was that — was that the time you sang your Death Song?" I could scarcely hear my own words for the hammering in my breast.

"That was later." His expression was a grotesque parody of Christian concern. "You must promise not to spook me again. A mossback old snapping turtle can take off your finger after you lop off its head."

I made him the promise. He slid his weight off me then. "Keep the crawlers to yourself, now. It's the ones come when your eyes are wide open you got to fear."

The warning was unnecessary. I slept no more.

The Black Hills accepted us the following morning without resistance, rather in the way that a spider knows no unwelcome visitors to its home — or so I interpreted in my combined states of agitation and exhaustion. Up close they were not black at all, but coated with dark ponderosa pines, grown so thickly that there were places where the sun had not been seen since the time of the glaciers. Our path was paved with a spongy layer, centuries in the making, of fallen needles over which hoofs and wheels passed without a sound. Indeed, the entire forest was eerily silent, yet far from uninhabited, and the very sight of those rows of trunks, together with the unnatural stillness of the air, made me imagine that I was standing on the edge of a pool of black water with no bottom, in danger of toppling in and sinking down and down into the icy inky depths where blind things swam about in absolute silence. Not sacred, these hills; damned.

"I didn't catch a wink that night for wondering if that breed was really dead or just foxing," Ben Wedlock said. That he had, without preamble, taken up his recollection of the night before where he had left off, made me jump. The sound of a human voice in that funereal treescape was as of a great bell rung in a deserted cathedral. "I snapped his neck, see, and there was no question but that the thing was done, and proper. But that don't cut water when you're alone with the sun gone and the stink of some squaw's bastard still up your nose. I bet I got up a hundred times to walk over and see was he still stretched out there, square on his back but looking at the ground, way his head was twisted.

"His pards come for me before dawn. I was in tall corn that summer from selling the freight business and I reckon them road agents seen me flashing the roll in town and followed me. Well, I gutted the first with my Green River knife and he was still twisting on the end of it when I shuck loose and throwed him at two more and tipped them over like lawn pins. I taken a ball in the meat of one arm then. It stung, so I laughed."

"You *laughed?*"

He nodded. "Stood there under the moon with blood shining on that knife and my own blood dripping off my fingers, laughing and bellering out 'I'm a Good Old Rebel,' all the verses I knowed plus a few more I made up and ain't for repeating here."

"What then?" said I, for he had paused, and I was caught up in the tale despite myself. Later I would represent that I was playing the wide-eyed youth in his thrall, as I had been charged. Thus was I my own dupe.

"Them highwaymen are all yellow. They expect folks they meet to be just as yellow as them. When they seen me standing there caterwauling square into Old Boneface like Ned's Crazy Uncle, it fair caught them up. Six on one it was, but here's the one winding himself up to take some down with him — and at night, yet, when scarecrows walk and Scratch brings in the harvest. Bandits is superstitious as niggers. Well, they fell back. I waited a little and then I got Old Deuteronomy out of the ravine where I had him tied and lit out before they changed their minds again. Barber dug the ball out of my arm and patched me up in Colorado Springs."

"You said Deuteronomy was killed at Second Manassas," I said, before I could catch myself.

"So I did, and so he was. I meant Nicodemus. Names and such all run together when you get to be my age."

I was relieved not to have unsettled him, for it was my responsibility not to let on that I knew him for a prevaricating scoundrel. And yet I was depressed by his slip, which had brought home to me the conviction that nothing he said was to be credited. Death Song indeed! He was as great an inventor as Judge Blod, who at least was not a bandit and murderer masquerading as a colorful old frontiersman. It occurred to me then that in the space of a few weeks I had fashioned rather more heroes than fell to the common lot of youth, only to see them crumble. I wished heartily that I had never heard of either Jed Knickerbocker or his half-dime dreadfuls.

"You're a quiet one today, Davy." Wedlock's eye was on Mr. Knox's wagon ahead. "I reckon old Ben spooked the tongue out of you last night."

"No," I said; and before he could fashion another, more dangerous explanation for my silence: "I was thinking about that Sioux policeman, Corporal Panther. Do you think he did what he said he would?"

"I didn't take him for a liar. He's bones by now, or soon will be."

"How do you know?"

"A bird told me." He pointed. High in the east, a great black vulture traced circles in the sky.

"It could be anything," I said. "A dead elk."

"Or a Panther."

I changed the subject. The vision of that splendid horseman lying stiff and cold and blind did not please me. "You said you prospected these hills once. Did you ever find gold?"

"Found some, not enough. Worked for it, too. Custer told the newspapers his horses was kicking up nuggets all over, but it weren't so. There was money to be made, but I was too lazy. Also I liked my scalp on top of my head and not swinging from some lodgepole."

"You don't want to be rich?"

"I got a business, a good horse even if he ain't Old Deuteronomy, and a friend or two amongst that flea-bit crowd back of us. How rich can you get?"

I believed then what Wedlock had told Deacon Hecate about himself and the church. No one who acknowledged the existence of God could say the things he said and not be constantly searching the heavens for signs of lightning.

A mule brayed at the rear of our procession, and for an instant I thought it *was* lightning. Someone shouted. I was off the wagon before Wedlock could set the brake. Ahead of us, Mr. Knox was reining in his team, and Judge Blod was just struggling down from his own seat behind the chuck wagon when I passed him running. I had an idea what I'd find. There was only one mule in our party.

A gang of riders made up mostly of Amarillo recruits had gathered behind the Judge's wagon. Mike McPhee had hold of Elder Sampson's big mule by the bit and was maneuvering his horse closer to avoid being torn out of his own saddle by the mule's plungings. The Elder lay on his face in the dirt. Long before I reached him I knew he was lost, for the back of his head had been laid open like an orange. I remember searching for a place to vomit, and finding it. I had never seen a man's brains before.

"What happened?" Deacon Hecate's voice was pure thunder. He towered tall and terrible astride his bony mare. His hat was off and his white hair whipped about in the wind.

"Cinch busted," Blackwater, who had dismounted, approached the Deacon carrying Elder Sampson's saddle. "I seen him fall. Reckon he hit his head on that rock."

The Deacon directed his predatory glare from the frayed end of the dangling cinch to the piece of shale that Blackwater had indicated on the ground near the body. "Indeed. And how came he to end up on his face?" He drew the yellow-handled pistol from under his coat and cocked it.

A very long silence followed. I stood crouched over my own bile in a patch of seedling pines beside the trail — disgraced, unarmed, and unable to come to his aid. Mr. Knox and Judge Blod had reached the scene on foot, hands inside their own coats, but judging by those concealed among the clothing of the others present, the Deacon had been correct in assuming that not everyone in the party had been disarmed at the outset. Even the wind died away, as if the Black Hills themselves were holding their breath.

It was Ben Wedlock, standing apart from the group with his thumbs in his belt, who broke the tension. "Blackwater, didn't your mother ever tell you a man's not to be moved until you know what ails him?"

The tall man with the feather in his hatband took the cigar out of his mouth and looked at the cold end. "Well, you're right, Ben. I turned him over before I knew what I was about."

"Impatient as ever, ain't it? Can't wait to start a thing before its time. What's your head for if not to keep your hat off your shoulders? I'm damned —" He seemed to realize suddenly that we were all watching him. Looking down at the body, he removed his hat. "Well, he's deader'n Prince Albert anyway. I don't reckon you damaged his case."

"Knox, inspect that cinch." Graven as was his expression, the Deacon swayed with the effort to check his fury.

Mr. Knox accepted the saddle from Blackwater and did as directed. "It has worn through and broken," he reported.

"We'd best bury him," said Wedlock,

tugging on his hat. "They bloat up quick in this heat."

Hecate swayed. Finally he took his pistol off cock. "You and you. Shovels." He pointed at Blackwater and McPhee, who had succeeded at last in calming the mule. The Irishman dismounted and the two went forward to Mr. Knox's wagon. "Back away, the rest of you. This is not a wolves' frenzy."

They buried Elder Sampson at the base of a hill, mounding the grave high and covering it with rocks to prevent coyotes from scratching up the remains, and fixed a cross made of pine boughs at its head. Deacon Hecate stood at the foot of the grave, his great white head bare and bowed.

"Seven sons and three daughters had Job," he said, and in his tone there was little of his customary thunder. "Friends and prosperity were his. But God was unsatisfied. To prove Job's loyalty, God permitted Satan to afflict him with boils, to impoverish him utterly, to slay his seven sons and three daughters. Later, as reward for Job's faith, God blessed his end more than his beginning. He gave him fourteen thousand sheep, and six thousand camels, and a thousand yoke of oxen, and a thousand she-asses. And Job had seven new sons and three new daughters."

For a long time he was silent. I thought the service had ended. Then he raised his long arms to the heavens; his head fell back, and on his face was an anguish I had never seen before. Indeed, I have not seen it anywhere since, although forty years have passed. His voice rose.

"But where, O God, are the seven sons and three daughters with whom Job started? What manner of heavenly grace can repay a life? What value loss, that it can be wiped away as with a damp cloth? I have not Job's patience, nor his great wisdom. I am sorely tried. Sorely tried. And I am not equal to the trial.

"*Smite* the evil that has claimed Thy son Schechaniah Sampson!" he shrieked. Every head came up. "Smite it low, that it shall not rise! Smite it with all Thy great might, or by the chaos that made Thee. Thy servant Philo shall seize that vengeance which is Thine, and though he crackle in Hell until Judgment, shall smite the evil himself if it means a cabal with Satan!"

This blasphemy was not lost upon even the group's most godless, for every man stood as if stricken throughout the Lord's

Prayer that incongruously followed, and those who had not yet forgotten the pious lessons of childhood crossed themselves. Long seconds after the Deacon had barked "Amen" and walked away to mount his mare, no one stirred.

"A crisis of faith," pronounced Judge Blod in a loud whisper. "I had not thought the two that close."

Mr. Knox said, "They weren't."

"Did the cinch really wear through?" I asked.

"There are ways to help it along, but the break appeared genuine. I doubt strongly that the rock was placed as conveniently as Blackwater claimed. Likely he saw his opportunity and acted, even if it meant upsetting Wedlock's timetable. Our saloonkeeper friend very nearly spilled the beans in his rage."

"What is our support?" asked the Judge.

"There in the Cheyenne party. I am uncertain of the fourth, and we know young Tom is lost."

"Not good."

"There is a bare possibility that today's incident will force Wedlock to begin early. However, I think he will wait until our quarry is assured. He's waited too many years to gamble upon our destroying all record of the gold's location on the very eve of victory."

"What is our plan?" I inquired, before the Judge could beat me to it.

Mr. Knox was grim. "There is no question but that the enemy has fired the first shot. It falls to us to fire the second. We move tonight."

15

Indians!

"Son, it's time."

There is a quarter hour, just before the first steel shaft parts the sky to the east, when the night loses its velvet gloss and becomes as flat and black as coke. It was in that quarter hour that Mr. Knox's words, whispered so close to my ear his lips almost touched it, brought me awake.

I was surprised to learn that I had lost consciousness at all with our plot about to unfold and its chief target lying only a yard away; but the sleep I had missed the previous night had caught up. I had left on my boots, and thanks to that ancient bed of pine needles managed to roll out and make away in Mr. Knox's footsteps without a sound.

Sleep now was as remote as Cathay,

there in the predawn Dakota chill with the birds mute in the trees and crickets stitching deep in the forest, as we crept past motionless blanketed figures — enemies all — toward our rendezvous. For the second time since we had entered these hills I felt poised on the edge of something. Was it just weeks ago that I had sat at my little desk, fretting over the rainfall in Argentina?

A crowd awaited us behind the wagon where the weapons were kept. At first I thought, with a tightening in my stomach, that the would-be mutineers had anticipated us, but then in the smoky starlight I recognized Judge Blod's rotundity and Deacon Hecate's angular height among three of the men whom the Deacon had drafted in Cheyenne. One, Will Asper, was a slim sandy youth, not ten years my senior and a contemporary of the treacherous Tom; the others, older, were an ox-shouldered Swede named Dahlgren — corrupted to Dolly by his peers — and a swarthy man, clean-shaven and balding in front, who was nearly Ben Wedlock's age and whose surname was Aintchell, although he was sometimes called H.L., which as pronounced by the Deacon sounded like "Angel." He seldom spoke and his eyes held a curious deadness I found unsettling. I understood that he had been a guard in the federal penitentiary at Yuma, Arizona, until a wave of humanitarian sentiment had forced officials there to replace its more brutal personnel. This was our army.

The Deacon issued pistols. I inspected the Navy Colt's load and thrust it inside my belt, feeling taller and older. Will Asper spun his balanced Russian like the gunmen Judge Blod wrote about, and Dolly wrapped a huge hand around a converted Army Colt's of Civil War vintage that obscured all but the end of its barrel. Aintchell dropped a short ugly bulldog revolver into his pocket after an indifferent glance and unfolded a fat jackknife to expose a blade with a wicked blue edge. He tested the point against the ball of one thumb. A drop of blood appeared. He licked it off.

"No unnecessary slaughter." The Deacon's low command seemed to be directed at Aintchell exclusively. "We shall want something to hang."

"Back in civilization," clarified Mr. Knox; "following a trial."

"Civilization is a world and a heaven away. Tonight we are fighting for our lives."

"*You're* fighting for your lives," Will Asper said. "What's our cut?"

"Equal parts of whatever we find. Which will amount to equal parts of nothing if we do not win tonight." Mr. Knox was emphatic.

Judge Blod said, "This is not a fit assignment for men of education and breeding. We should send Master Grayle for help."

Thus were the Judge's true colors hoisted at last. Mr. Knox ignored them, twirling the cylinder of his pocket Lightning.

"Even if he made it, he would return to find us all murdered. You all know the plan. Deacon, you and the others will throw down on the Amarillans and our two recalcitrants from Cheyenne. David, the horses are your responsibility. If anyone makes for them, run them off. They won't wander far, and we cannot afford to let any of Wedlock's men ride back for reinforcements. Wedlock is mine."

"I claim Wedlock," said the Deacon.

"We shall go together. That puts you in charge of the others, Judge. Remember, no shooting unless they produce a weapon."

"Or knifing." This time there was no question that the Deacon was addressing Aintchell, who shrugged as he wiped his blade rhythmically on his shirt.

Mr. Knox said, "You have five minutes to reach your stations. When I fire my pistol, that will be the signal to act."

"You best fire it now, schoolteacher."

None of us had observed Mike McPhee gliding through the shadows, and now he stood ten paces away with his back to the camp and the first gray streaks of dawn shining on his drawn pistol, a small instrument of the pocket variety like Mr. Knox's, but with a larger bore. His loud brogue rang in the morning stillness.

"If you ain't fixing to fire it," he said, "maybe you best toss it back with the rest. Now." He cocked his weapon for emphasis.

Mr. Knox let out his breath, half turned, and tossed his pistol into the wagon with a clatter.

"Unburden yourselves, the rest of you. That goes for the brat."

Judge Blod was the first to obey. Deacon Hecate opened his stern mouth as if to deliver an oration from Scripture, then seemed to think better of it and added his yellow-handled pistol to the pile in the wagon. This prompted Will Asper and Dolly to relinquish their arms. I surrendered the Navy. Aintchell alone hesitated. In the growing light, McPhee's face grew dangerous. "You too, Fisheye. That short piece in your pocket."

Aintchell drew out the bulldog revolver carefully and flipped it with a nonchalant movement into the wagon.

"Try to get the better of Bloody Bill's men, is it? You'll learn —"

Turning back, Aintchell made a little sidearm gesture as if sweeping open a door. The Irishman's reactions were fast. He fired and Aintchell doubled over. But not before McPhee reeled back with the black handle of the jackknife standing out like a stud from the center of his chest. Correcting himself automatically, he lurched forward a step, then stumbled back two and sat down hard on the ground, losing his grip on the pistol. His face was in shadow now and I could not imagine its expression. After a moment he heeled over.

By this time Aintchell was in convulsions on the ground, both hands clutching his belly. A hideous stench of blood and excrement and spent powder fouled the morning air.

There was, however, no time to see to him. "Quickly, now!" barked Mr. Knox, reaching back inside the wagon. With startled obscenities the camp was coming alive around us. I moved to join him. Irrationally, I groped for my own weapon in the darkness, ignoring all others. The Deacon shoved me aside to capture the instrument most handy, after which there was a scramble.

"On the ridge!"

The Judge's baritone was nearly as loud as McPhee's shot. In my excitement I applauded him, imagining that his wits had overcome his native cowardice and that he had sung out to distract the raiders while we established our position. A sudden stillness among my fellow defenders killed that thought. The entire camp, in fact, had fallen silent except for the mortal groans of the wounded Aintchell at our feet. I withdrew my hands from the arsenal and followed the others' gaze to the high ground in the east, where the sun was rising behind a line of mounted men crowned with feathers and painted barbarically from hairlines to moccasins.

They capped the horizon, looking as tall as the sparse evergreens that studded that rocky slope and nearly as inanimate, only their feathers and plaited hair moving in the wind. It seemed at first that there were hundreds. In truth they were but a score.

In that moment I realized the tales I had read in the Knickerbocker books, of handfuls of plucky frontiersmen standing off hordes of redskins, were not so much outright lies as innocent exaggerations. Fear is the great multiplier.

The odds were sufficiently daunting. Drawn together though we now were by race and mutual survival, without McPhee and Aintchell we were just fourteen, and they held the high ground with rifles and carbines in hand and the sun in our eyes. They wore, in addition to the traditional savage regalia, white men's cotton shirts with the sleeves torn off and simple geometric designs painted on in bright colors — the "ghost shirts" of infamy. I did not doubt that this was Lives Again and his band of renegades from Standing Rock; flushed with their late victory over their pursuers, serene in the belief that their charmed tunics would preserve them from harm, the taste of Corporal Panther's blood still upon their tongues. In my mind's eye I saw a cadre of vultures circling over my own poor remains.

Still they did not move. It seemed hours. It was probably moments. I began to hope . . .

"Tom, no!"

Ben Wedlock's shout brought me around just as he lunged to slap aside the barrel of our young traitor's rifle. In that instant it discharged. Dirt and pebbles spattered one of the horses on the hill. The animal blew and reared. While its rider struggled for control — a war-horse it most decidedly was not — another brave leveled his carbine across his own mount's neck and fired. Tom cried out and fell.

There would be no peace that day. More shots followed, whether from our side or theirs I cannot say now and could not tell then, for in the next moment the fighting became general. With brain-curdling whoops and cries the riders charged down the slope, firing under and over their horses' necks and maneuvering the animals at full gallop between and around rocks and trees as if one brain controlled both horse and rider. Now and then in my sleep I still hear bullets whizzing past me and wake up shouting.

For me, the fight lasted less than a minute. I have spent many hours dissecting those movements I witnessed and was part of, and have concluded that there were at least twenty. I saw the Deacon, as erect as on those Sundays when he read from the Book of Genesis to all who would listen, steadying his pistol across one forearm and firing in a precise hammering rhythm, with measured spaces between shots; Eli Freedman unlashing the team belonging to Judge Blod's wagon and shooting one of the animals so beloved of him to create a breastwork; the Judge's ample backside retreating toward a part of that country not overrun by Indians; Christopher Agnes whirling a sack of snakes around his head and letting fly into the arms of a startled Indian bearing down upon him. These things I saw and more, despite Mr. Knox's attempts to push me under the wagon while fending off attackers with the pistol in his other hand. Eventually he became too involved in the latter activity, and I moved away from his protection.

I do not know to this day whether it was a bullet that clipped me or the butt of a long gun, for it was in the nature of those Indians to use their firearms as bludgeons when they were among us. I remember taking aim at a human being for the first time in my life, and I remember that by some miracle I had managed after all to snatch my inherited Navy from the pile. I remember too that my target was a superbly ugly creature with his face painted in halves of black and vermilion, busy closing in upon a distracted Will Asper. After that I remember nothing except an explosion of pain and sudden nausea, followed by a black void.

16

Mad Alice

Reality was a slow dawning through a gauzy window. I lay without moving, seeing objects around me without registering their place or function, while a slothful kind of panic spread through me, of time lost and an appointment of mortal importance missed. So potent was this fear that for minutes I did not notice the pain in my head. When I raised it, lightning arced, blinding me. I fell back with a gasp. A cushion fashioned from some scratchy material sewn inside scratchy material supported my head. I was in a bed of some kind. Mine? Had I, in one of the periodic fevers that swept through my place and time, merely *dreamed* all of the events from Jotham Flynn on? Would my mother at any moment enter with her unspeakable soup and assure me that all was as it had al-

186

ways been? I cannot say now whether this information would have relieved or distressed me.

"Calvin, you never will learn to duck when that crazy piebald scoots under the apple tree."

The voice, an aural personification of the creaking inside my head, broke into a wheezy cackle. Decidedly it did not belong to my mother. Out of the corner of one eye I saw a figure seated beside the bed that I will not at this point describe, for fear the reader will think me un-recovered from the blow to my head. I was not certain myself.

"Swallow this." A crusty hand stole behind my neck, supporting it as a black spoon that had once been silver came to my lips.

The odor that filled my nostrils from the liquid in the bowl of the spoon was indescribable, but not unpleasant; and warm. Emphatically, it did not remind me of my mother's sickbed brew. My stomach growled then and I realized that much time had passed since it had held anything. Obediently I opened my mouth. The flavor was familiar and welcome; a meat broth. Greedily I accepted another spoonful and yet another. No feast was ever appreciated more. I asked what it was. My own voice was nearly as creaky as the one that answered.

"Venison and something that fell in the pot while I was stirring. I don't think it was a rat. Lizard, likely. Drink up, Calvin. There's more where it came from."

I declined politely. The explanation had added more ominous noises to those already issuing from my insides. "Who is Calvin?" I asked.

Cackle. "You're who's Calvin, boy! I guess that piebald fetched you up proper. Sleep's the cure. You just lay back now and let Mother see to your chores."

Trying to make sense of the things she said did little for my headache. I think I did sleep. In any case, when next I opened my eyes, the cabin was in darkness.

I say "cabin." In truth it was a dugout affair with rounded walls smelling richly of earth, logs laid across the front, and a square of buckskin hanging over what I presumed was the entrance. These things I remember from my first awakening, for they were shadowed now beyond the reach of a rude tallow lamp burning greasily upon a pedestal table of eastern manufacture. Between it and my bed, noisily asleep with its mouth open in a warped rocking chair, sat the creature who had addressed me as Calvin.

This, I had divined, was female, although little about its appearance suggested the gender. Tiny it was — Judge Blod would have seemed a giant next to it — wrapped in a short hide jacket whose sleeves came almost to its fingertips and a skirt of some sturdy dark material, beneath which poked a pair of man's brogans worn nearly transparent in the toes. They would be concealed completely when the figure stood. At the other end, under a hat with a narrow flat brim overgrown with faded artificial flowers, a comical face with a bulbous nose performed as trumpet for a remarkable scale of snores. Dirty yellow hair slanted down under the hat's brim all around, like shocked corn.

This collection would have lifted eyebrows anywhere. I thought of illustrations I had seen in children's books of gnomes and trolls who dwelt beneath bridges and challenged the right of wayfarers to pass over. But I knew now that she was real; just as I knew, with a sickening sensation of guilt, that through capricious fate I had been spared the destiny of my companions, whose scalps by now were certainly decorating the lances of Lives Again's renegades.

Today, whenever I suffer the discomforts of age, I like to remember the night I raised myself from bed with what was probably at least a mild concussion, wanting desperately to drift back into seductive sleep but wanting more (with no real idea of what I would do once I got there) to return to the place where I had left Mr. Knox, Judge Blod, Deacon Hecate, and the others in the midst of savages. Blood sloshed inside my head, made heavy by a coarse bandage wound several times around it. Twice I nearly lost consciousness. Once I lost my balance and fell against the pedestal table, upsetting the lamp and causing the old woman to stir in her sleep and say something that was not much less comprehensible than the things she said when she was awake. I righted the lamp and lowered stockinged feet to a floor of icy bedrock. She had removed only my boots, and these I found when I stepped on one at the foot of the bed. I picked them up and crept unsteadily on the balls of my feet toward the buckskin flap.

The air outside was cold but dry. Under a tattered moon the familiar rounded shapes of the Black Hills crawled against a charcoal sky. That much was comforting, although I did not know from which direction I was looking at them or whether I was scant yards or several miles away from the place where I had seen them last. Where to go?

Even in my foggy state I knew that it did not matter where I went if I did not have a horse under me. Surely the old woman's poor brogans could not carry her the distances she would have to travel to survive in that wilderness; nor could someone of her diminutive stature have carried me very far on foot. I looked for a stable, and found one. A poor thing it was, constructed of crooked poles arranged in a stockade against a pile of fallen rocks with a roof intended more to provide shade from the sun than for protection from rain and snow, but I detected restless movement between the poles and heard a shuddering snort. I pulled on my boots and started that way.

I tripped on something, barking a shin, and threw out a hand to break my fall. Halfway down it grasped something rigid. Pushing myself erect, I saw that I was standing in a patch of wooden crosses, one of which had arrested my descent. There were five, each protruding above an oblong mound of stones. I had stumbled into a small graveyard. I felt a chill. Were these victims of the old woman, and was a sixth cross intended for me?

Circling the patch hurriedly, I undid a crude latch and stepped through a door into manure-sodden darkness. A large animal blew and shifted its weight. Very slowly my eyes adjusted to the moonlight sifting in between the poles overhead. The first thing I saw clearly was a man stretched out on the ground at my feet.

I lunged backward, bumping the back of my bandaged head against the door. A red wash obscured my vision; again I almost fell, and clutched at a pole for support. The enclosure swayed. The animal wickered and fiddlefooted to the opposite side.

"Please don't do that again. I have not come this far to be trampled to death."

In my delirium the voice sounded familiar. As my sight returned — more slowly than the first time — I saw in the striped moonlight that the supine figure wore a cavalry tunic over leggings. Above it, one eye rolling white, stood a fine big tawny drayhorse, very old. The man appeared at first to be lying comfortably with his hands laced behind his head, but then I saw that they were tied with a thong to one of the poles that supported the roof. His hair was long and dark and unfettered.

"Corporal Panther?" I whispered. This, I knew, was the proper tone in which to address a ghost.

"Who are you?" There was hope and suspicion in his voice, most unghostlike.

"David Grayle. I am — was — with Deacon Hecate's party. Are you alive?"

"The prospectors. I remember." Irony now. "I have not passed over just yet. Was?"

"We were set upon by renegades. I woke up here. The others —" I changed the subject. "We thought you were dead."

"I thought the same thing when my horse was shot out from under me."

I knew now why the vulture had been circling. "Lives Again?"

"Mad Alice."

"Who?"

"The old woman. Star-Touched Woman, she is called among the Sioux. I've heard stories about her all my life. I assumed she was long dead."

"Who is she?"

"No one knows, really. The whites call her Mad Alice but if she even remembers her right name she's never been heard to use it. They say she came out here in the fifties in a wagon with her husband and three children. Blackfeet slaughtered the others, raped her, and left her to die, but she fooled them and survived. By then she was crazy, or maybe she always was. Crow warriors built the dugout and this stable to please the Great Spirit, who favors the insane. I imagine this old nag is another bit of tribute, stolen as a colt from some long-gone farming family. How she's lived this long is beyond me. Maybe the Crow were right."

"She called me Calvin."

"That's the name on one of the graves outside," he said. "I saw that much while she was marching me in here at the point of a musket as old as my father. She must think you're one of her dead sons. That explains why you're not trussed up."

"Why are you?"

"The Sioux and Blackfeet are old enemies. She seems to think the Blackfeet are holding her family and that she can bargain for their release by offering to turn me over for torturing. That's when she remembers me at all. When she put her horse in here yesterday and saw me she almost shot me. I had to remind her of her plan."

"What if she goes through with it?"

"There haven't been any Blackfeet in

this country for years. I'll starve to death before she gives me to them. She hasn't fed me in days."

He sounded desperately weak. I saw then that his coat was stained and that the wound in his side had broken open. "You're bleeding!"

"Never mind that. See if you can untie me."

I bent and worked at the knot. The thong was made of rawhide and I scratched at it with my nails until they bled. Finally he said, "You'll have to cut it."

"I haven't a knife."

"Get one from the dugout.

I paused. "She's in there."

"That's no problem for a loving son."

I stared at him, but there was no trace of humor in the Indian features. I straightened and left the stable.

The old woman was still snoring fearsomely. In silence I lowered the buckskin flap behind me, retrieved the tallow lamp, and conducted a search on tiptoe of the dugout. This did not take long. It was scrupulously neat for an earthen construction and contained only the bed, her chair, the table, a barrel of meat packed in salt, some scorched pots under the smokehole where a fire had burned recently inside a circle of rocks, a home-made broom, and a chest of drawers suggestive of some eastern parlor, but which had dried and cracked for lack of oil. Inside the drawers, amidst an incongruous conglomeration of silver-backed hairbrushes, sacks of black powder, button hooks, hidescrapers, jewelry, and fifty-caliber musket balls, I found my Navy Colt's and the leathern sack containing the Confederate note with Jotham Flynn's map sketched on the end. I stared at the last in the flickering light. Recent events had chased all thoughts of Yankee treasure from my mind. Finally I returned the note to the sack, pocketed it, selected a paring knife with a chipped bone handle from among the utensils in the top drawer, and thrust it and the pistol inside my belt. I turned to go.

"Calvin, you bad boy. How many times have I told you not to play with things that don't belong to you?"

So caught up was I in my search I had failed to notice that Mad Alice had stopped snoring. Now I faced the tiny old woman, standing bright-eyed behind a flintlock musket with a bore as big around as a fifty-cent piece. And then, studying me closely, she squinted one eye and said three words that scant hours ago I would not have believed could chill me as much as they did.

"You ain't Calvin."

17

The Fifth Grave

I had, I confess, a sudden urge to deny her assertion. The ancient weapon was fearsome, and life as her son appeared more gratifying than the prospect of my entrails ornamenting the earthen walls of her home. However, mad though she may have been, to assume stupidity on her part as well could have been instantly fatal.

I said, "My name is David Grayle. I am a prospector."

"I remember. I scraped you off the ground with a ditch alongside your head deep enough to strike water. At the time I thought you was my boy. Renegade white, I expect. Nobody prospects these hills, two yards deep in Blackfeet. That your tribe?" The musket twitched. I had no doubt what an answer in the affirmative would bring.

"My party was attacked by Indians. You must have seen that a fight had taken place."

"I seen sign." Memory grappled with her demented state for control of her face. "Sure, there was a dead one close by."

My chest constricted. "An Indian?"

"White. Who was it done the attacking, Blackfeet?"

In my anguish over which of my companions she had found slain, I very nearly made the response I sensed she wished to hear. At the last instant I said, "No, I think they were Sioux."

Immediately I realized how close I had come to annihilation; for after a pause she lowered the musket, keeping the hammer in firing position. "I smelt Sioux. You said Blackfeet, I'd of knowed you was one of them. These here times you can't be too . . ."

Her voice lost definition. The room spun and the bedrock floor opened beneath me.

When my vision returned, I was back in bed. Mad Alice was in her chair. There was concern in her humorous features. The room had lightened and I knew that I had slept away the night at least. I wondered, with the sudden clarity of understanding that sometimes comes upon awakening, if to her I was her boy Calvin once again, and that I would have to go through the same process a second time. Her first words laid that fear to rest.

"Them Sioux is almost as bad as Blackfeet. I guess they scrambled your skull fair."

I did not tell her that she had been more responsible than the Sioux for this latest lapse. "What are you going to do with me?" I asked.

"My question. The Christian thing, I expect. I ain't been in these hills so long I turned heathen. You'll earn it back when you're on your feet. The woodshed needs filling."

"What about Corporal Panther?"

"Corporal Who?"

"The man in the stable."

"What do you know about a man in the stable?"

The harsh question told me I had made a mistake. However, having learned that the way to get on with her was to tell the truth at all times, I explained, "I went out and spoke with him when you were asleep before. I know him. He is a policeman from the Sioux reservation at Standing Rock. He represents no harm to you."

"You're right on that. I mean to trade

him for my husband Charlie and our three boys."

"They're dead."

"Blackfeet took them for ransom last month," she said dreamily. "They'll admire to have a strong young Sioux buck to hoist and skin slow. I'll deliver him and some powder and balls and something else and they'll give me back Charlie and Calvin and George and little Charlie Junior."

It occurred to me that at no time was she entirely lucid. In addition to believing that the occupants of the graves outside were still alive and captives of the long-departed Blackfeet, she had obliterated more than thirty years from her memory, imagining that the tragedy had taken place only weeks before. She would require cautious handling.

Said I, "He is worth nothing to them dead. He has not been fed nor his wound seen to."

"I ain't got time to patch up no redskin, and if I had the time I wouldn't have the victuals to spare. There's no corner markets in the Black Hills."

"I cannot answer for the state of your provisions. As for time, it is one thing I have in plenty." This was the first lie I had told her. I was in a fever to know what had become of Mr. Knox, Judge Blod, and the rest.

She cackled. "You can't see to yourself, leave off anyone else."

"That is my worry, and one less for you if I die in the attempt. But if the Indian dies, so too will your hopes of ever seeing your family again. We can share rations," I added.

She chewed over the proposition; or rather, made the motion of doing so, for I had already determined she had no teeth. The chair creaked as she rocked. Then she stopped and pushed herself to her feet. "I'd best get to stewing."

"I will gather wood." I got out of bed, more carefully than the first time. The pain in my head had subsided to a noisy throbbing. I noticed upon standing that this time she had left me my boots, while relieving me of the revolver and paring knife.

Evidently my actions betrayed this discovery, for she said, "I put them away for you. I don't guess you need them to gather wood." Cackling gently, she began stirring one of her pots, the contents of which — the rat or lizard soup, I assumed — appeared to have gone viscous.

I left the dugout without comment.

Plainly, I had not yet found her depth.

The bright sunshine felt good after the chill damp of that man-made cave, but it did little for my spirits. One at least of my party was dead, and possibly all of them, while I lived; a boy who had thought himself a man but who when it came to a reckoning had proved to be something considerably less. I knew not where I was in that wild land, and had I known, possessed no idea of what I could do to correct the situation. Less understandably, I felt low for having used an old woman's delusions to my credit. Certainly it was not my fault that her family was dead, but it seemed poor coin for her having saved my life.

For all that, escape was very much in my thoughts. Uncertainty as to how much Mad Alice had suspected of my motives in securing the knife and pistol did not stay me from heading straight for the stable and making off with the drayhorse. Thought of Corporal Panther did. To leave now would be to sentence him to death by starvation or from the evils of an uncared-for wound.

I wanted to go into the stable immediately, but was aware that the dugout's door flap was ajar and that the old woman was watching me. Instead I went through the open end of a lean-to made from the same kind of poles that supported the stable roof, braced against the entrance to the dugout, and picked up an armload of wood, chopped in lengths of about eighteen inches and well seasoned. This I carried inside and deposited under the smokehole, where I commenced to lay a fire. Mad Alice meanwhile had abandoned her post at the door to carve long strips off a portion of salted meat from the barrel, which she then transferred to the pot along with water from a hide bag of Indian manufacture. That done, she set aside the pot, produced flint and steel, and using dead grass for kindling started a flame burning inside the circle of rocks. With the aid of an ironwood trivet held together with pegs of the same sturdy material, she set the pot's contents cooking. Before long the familiar indescribable aroma filled the dugout.

By the time she tasted and pronounced the stew ready, I was famished, but asked permission to take a bowl to Corporal Panther.

"Suit yourself," she said. "There's one way in and out of the stable and I'll be watching it with my musket."

This was as near as she came to voicing a threat. I said, "I shall need bandaging material and alcohol to cleanse his wound."

"Curtain cloth's in there." She indicated the chest of drawers. "Charlie and me don't hold with spirits."

"Soap and water, then."

She reached inside one of the pockets of her hide jacket and handed me a shapeless white lump made from pure fat with something added to give it a gritty texture. "Fill the bag after. Crick's behind the stable."

I felt her watching me on my way to Panther's berth and so did not tarry by the little graveyard. There was a thing about it that bothered me, but which had nothing to do with the terrible circumstances that had created it.

The Indian was in a bad way. There were flies on his closed lashes and when I opened the stable door I smelled corruption. The flies buzzed around when he opened his eyes.

"I smell food." His voice was so hoarse it was almost nonexistent.

Arranging my articles on the packed earth floor, I knelt and supported the back of his head with one hand while placing the spoon to his lips. He accepted its contents as eagerly as I had earlier. After several more swallows, he said, "I thought I'd been deserted."

"The old woman caught me. I couldn't get the knife."

"She is half tough."

"More than half. I must get to your wound."

"I'm in no position to stop you." He flexed his bound hands.

I spread his coat. The blood from the deep laceration in his side had crusted black, making it difficult to tell where the flesh left off and his breechclout began. I tore a piece from the curtain material I had brought, splashed water onto it, and rubbed it with soap until I had a semblance of lather.

"I haven't alcohol or peroxide," I warned him. "It means scrubbing."

"Talk to me."

I knew his meaning. The dried blood was stubborn and he took in his breath. "It smells of infection," I said. "I can clean away the worst and patch you up, but you must see a doctor soon."

"Talk about something else." He was gnawing his lip.

"I have been wondering about something you said, about Mad Alice's family. You said her husband and three sons were killed."

"That's the story I heard."

"She confirmed it. She won't admit they're dead, but the number is the same, four. Why are there five graves?"

"Are there five?"

I nodded. The last of the old blood had come away. The flesh around the wound had a reddish tinge much brighter than its natural pigment, a bad sign. I tore the rest of the material into long strips.

"Maybe she filled one herself," he said. "She is no poor hand with that museum piece."

"I doubt she would have buried a slain enemy next to her family." I wound the first of the strips around his abdomen and fixed a patch against the torn flesh.

"Maybe they're all enemies. Maybe she buried her family somewhere else."

"Why bury an enemy at all?"

"This is Mad Alice we're discussing," he reminded me. "Who is to say what goes on in her head?"

I tied off the bandage. "There seems to be a good deal of sanity in her madness."

"I would not know. All I know of her is what you can see strapped belly-down over the saddle of that monster. That's how she brought me here."

As if understanding that it had been referred to, the ancient drayhorse stamped a hoof and snuffled. Thus far it had kept its distance, possibly because of the stenches of blood and infection still in the air. Horses shy from mortality.

"It is of no consequence," I said. "I shall keep trying for that knife. We must be away from here."

"Don't take too long about it, David."

It was the first time he had addressed me by name. That, and the look in his frank dark eyes there in the striped sunlight, caused me to assure him that I would not.

As I left the stable, carrying the bowl of stew and the water bag and soap, I felt something in my pocket. I balanced the bowl in the crook of my left arm and drew out the leathern pouch. With just the Confederate note inside, it had lain flat against my hip, and so the old woman had overlooked it when she took away my other contraband a second time. I did not move from the spot. Standing facing the Black Hills at that angle, holding the map that Orrin Peckler had made, and for which Jotham Flynn had killed him, I stared from one to the other and then at the five graves clustered between the stable and the dugout.

And then I knew.

18

Freedom,
After a Fashion

There was nothing I could do, of course, about my newfound knowledge, even had I wanted to. Mad Alice was watching my movements, and anyway my only wish was to be away from there with Panther and on the trail of what remained of my party.

As I descended the slope behind the stable that led to a rusty creek, my thoughts turned to the practical. I could easily overpower the old woman, but the fact that she *was* old, and consequently brittle, forced me to consider that course of action a last resort. With my friends' plight weighing upon my conscience I scarcely needed to add the serious injury or death of an elderly widow whose addled condition was her only crime. My own brain was not much better, owing both to the complexity of my situation and to the thudding in my head. My emotions were as numb as my hands where the icy mountain water flowed over them on its way into the hide bag.

They remained so for the better part of that day. I ate, napped, listened to Mad Alice's ravings about nonexistent Indians, fetched wood, napped, delivered straw to the old horse in the stable, fed Panther from my own rations and inspected his bandages, napped some more. I could not get enough sleep. It was as if all the hours I had lost so far in my great adventure had been waiting in ambush, and yet the more I slept the more exhausted I felt. I know now that I was suffering from deep shock. It is no small thing for a boy to face events that make grown men throw up their hands and turn to the wall. Of all the things that happened to me and about me during that unforgettable season, the days and nights I spent with the old woman seem the most like a childhood dream.

Dusk of that day brought opportunity. After freshening the stew with shavings from the salted meat, Mad Alice laid down her knife to return the meat to its barrel and left the knife lying atop the cracked chest of drawers. I tried not to stare at it as she stirred the stew. Had she forgotten to put it away, or was it part of some test? The swiftness with which she had gone from unconscious fixture to armed sentinel the previous night had left me wondering about that episode as well; there was no fathoming the workings of her uncategorable mind. If I seized the instrument, would she take the action for a threat, snatch up the musket that was never more than an arm's length away, and make a stew of me also? The phrase, occurring to me merely as a colorful play on words, set me thinking wildly. How much, after all, did I know about her nature? I had heard hideous stories about what happened to people alone and starving in the wilderness. Was the meat in the barrel actually venison, or the grisly fate of some innocent wayfarer who like Panther had wandered unwittingly inside range of her weapon? Had she indeed taken me in and begun fattening me for reasons other than Christian? My emotions, thawing, were uncoiling themselves in confusion. I realized suddenly that the old woman was staring at me.

"You fixing to grow sprouts or what? I'll need wood."

I made my decision. The curtain material I had not used in dressing Panther's wound remained on the chest of drawers where I had left it, a fortunate turn. "The Indian's bandages will require changing by now. May I do that first?"

"I swear you put more store by that savage than your own belly. Don't forget the wood. Or who's watching you," she added, squinting.

I mumbled something to the effect that I would forget neither and gathered up the material, and with it the knife. My head was pounding in counterpoint to my heart as I approached the door flap.

"Hey, boy," said Mad Alice.

I faltered. Run, or make my stand? The time for last resorts had arrived. I turned, bracing myself to leap. If her arm was faster . . .

She had picked up the rough soap and water bag and was holding it out. I hesitated, relief washing up and over me like a warm tide, and stepped forward to take them.

Knowing that she was watching from the doorway, I took my time during the trek past the graveyard. I was very conscious of the knife wrapped in the net cloth. By the time I was inside the stable, I was wrapped in a sheath of cold sweat like a clammy shroud. The smell of it caused the old horse to back away from me.

Panther was alert. Quickly I set about removing his old dressing and flushing the wound. I was glad to see the red patch had not spread. He sensed my excitement. There was a question in his eyes. Grinning like the schoolboy I was, I produced the knife. It had a Sheffield blade and a hide handle that had replaced the broken or worn-out original. In a trice I had sawed through his bonds and he sat rubbing his wrists.

"She is watching the door," I said. "We must wait our chance."

"I've been waiting longer than you. It is now or never."

"Mad Alice —"

"She can fire that musket only once before reloading. Give me the knife."

He took it away while I was considering the request. "You are too weak," I said. "She will cut you down long before you get —"

"I am too close to death to start attacking old ladies now." He shifted positions, grunting a little, and commenced sawing with the edge of the blade at the leather thongs that held together the poles from which the wall was made. "Get ready to catch these before they can fall outward," he said. "We haven't time for a saddle and bridle. Can you ride bareback?"

"I can try."

"That means you cannot. But if you can boost me aboard we can both try. Here comes the first."

I grasped the pole just as the last thong encircling it fell away and drew it inside, leaning it against the front wall by the door. He was already working at the next. "Hurry," said I. "She is sure to wonder what's keeping me."

"If I work any faster I will start losing fingers."

The effort was tiring him already. Without a word I took the knife from his hand — he offered little resistance — and cut through the remaining thongs while he rested. I caught the poles myself and leaned them next to the first. We now had an opening on the blind side of the dugout.

Panther said, "That's enough. Help me up."

"One more pole."

"Leave it. We'll manage. Get moving!"

The Indian was heavier than he looked, but I helped him to his feet and after two tries, over the back of the horse, which snorted and shambled but found no escape inside the small enclosure. I got on behind, not without difficulties of my own. The animal was all bone and sagging flesh; straddling it was like sitting on loose floating logs. However, it supported our combined weight without great effort.

"Ready?" said Panther. Before I could reply, he dug in his heels and we shot through the opening.

It was a tight fit. The rough poles on either side tore my trousers and took skin off my legs. I reeled, surprised by the pain and our jolting start; reflex alone kept me in my seat as I swept both arms about Panther's waist, forcing a grunt from him because of his wound. Outside, the fresh air of freedom struck with flatiron force.

Out of the corner of one eye I glimpsed a familiar flower-hatted figure poised halfway between dugout and stable. Something split the air past my head with a loud crack. She had brought her musket with her.

I paid no attention to our course, trusting to the Indian and disregarding his pain as I hugged him for life and liberty. Either the old workhorse was faster than it appeared or I was drunk with motion, but it seemed that we were flying. The hammering of hoofs outdid the pounding in my head. Wind buffeted my ears.

We were free — or as free as befell a half-dead Sioux and a battered white youth without arms or provisions in the treacherous Black Hills of South Dakota.

19

The Way to Death

Night fell quickly in that hill country, and we had gone a very little distance before darkness forced us to halt. The activity had deeply taxed Panther's weakened constitution. I helped him down, made a bed in the lee of a wash from pine needles and plucked grass, plucked more with which to rub down the winded and disgruntled old workhorse, and used my belt to tether it to a juniper. Then I huddled close to the Indian. It was a cold night and very long.

Panther was worse at dawn. When I helped him to his feet he was barely conscious, and although he had not bled through his bandages, his forehead was hot, indicating that the fever was in his blood. Helping him aboard our bleary-eyed mount, I knew that he would not survive another night without medical help.

For what it was worth, I now knew how to get back to where I had left Mr. Knox and the rest. Whatever his shortcomings as a Union Army paymaster, Orrin Peckler was an able cartographer and had faithfully recorded the landmarks that surrounded us on his makeshift map. With the sun's position as my guide I turned the horse's head to the southwest, and with my arms around the sagging Indian and grasping the mane, and using my knees and heels, started us along the path of least resistance. For sanity's sake I did not allow myself to think about what we might — or might not — find at the end of our journey.

The day was blistering. I had had the foresight to bring along the water bag, but even so we stopped often in the shade of the pines to cool our bodies and let the horse blow. Panther was now alert, now nearly comatose. He was actually easier to manage in the latter state, for when his senses were about him he would argue that we were headed in the wrong direction for salvation, that I must give up my friends as lost and set a course for Standing Rock. I knew not where Standing Rock was or how long I could depend upon him to guide me, and so I ignored his protests. Fortunately, he hadn't the strength to override me.

Or perhaps unfortunately; but again I am outdistancing myself.

The sky was broad and blue and polished painfully bright. High above the hills an eagle (I preferred not to think it was a vulture) slid between clouds upon spread wings, flapping them now and again only to climb higher before diving hundreds of feet into the next updraft — mocking, it seemed to me, our ants' progress along the uneven ground. Other, lesser birds whistled and squawked in the trees and squirrels repelled down the trunks and scudded across the forest floor with the noise of crashing elk. The plenitude of the game, unarmed as I was, served only to remind me of the gnawing in my stomach. I began to think nostalgically about Mother's sickbed soup.

Mother. What was she doing now back in Panhandle? If it was Monday, she would be washing the linen and airing out the mattresses; Tuesday, scouring the floors with the harsh soap that bleached the boards and made her knuckles swell and crack; Wednesday, shopping in town for the corned beef whose fat melted like

219

butter on the tongue and milk by the pail, still foaming from the cow's heat, and if there was a boarder, canned peaches or apricots, served chilled from the icebox and so sweet they hurt the teeth; Thursday or Friday, the windows; Saturday, sewing, her fingers working as fast as any bobbin as she replaced buttons, repaired rents, pieced together my shirts and the dresses she fashioned from bright prints to look her prettiest for the male roomers she admired; Sunday, coming back from church to fill the house with the warm sunny smell of baking bread. I smelled it now, and I saw her face, and unashamedly I wept, the boy who would be a man, stranded in strange country with a dying Indian and an ancient horse and a numbness inside that passed for hope.

I felt loneliest when our way took us through forest so deep that nothing grew and consequently no animals lived, where the dense trunks did for night and silence spread around us like a brackish pool. My skin, so recently slick with sweat, grew cold and clammy and I shivered uncontrollably. The horse sensed my unease and shied from the sound of its own hoofbeats. I took what heat I could from Panther, who by then was burning up with fever and muttering deliriously in his semiconscious state. Of what he spoke I was for the most part ignorant, for it was mainly in a language that I assumed was Sioux. Once only did he raise his voice clearly in English, and I wished that he had not, because the words left me colder than the forest shadows.

"The white man's road," he said, "is the way to death." After that he lapsed back into his native tongue.

The sun was growing rusty when we passed out of a narrow cleft between hills whose steep faces rose like cliffs on either side and into a clearing I recognized with my insides before my mind caught up. The horse recognized it too, and the memory was not good, because it threw up its head and whistled through its nostrils and tried to rear. Its old muscles were not equal to its heart, however, and before it could pitch us off I slid to the ground and brought Panther tumbling down with me, breaking his fall as best I could with my own body. He sank down with a grunt. I made sure, first, that he was still breathing, then that he was in a relatively comfortable position in the tall grass, and turned to try and soothe the big drayhorse. Clearly my priorities were in faulty order. It had wheeled and was retreating the way we had come at a gallop several times faster than I had managed to get it into thus far. It would not stop running until it was safely back in its own stable.

The animal's panic had not been entirely the result of memory. When with an air of resignation I turned back to see to the Indian, I saw, not thirty yards away, what at first appeared to be a pile of discarded clothing lying, as Panther was lying, in the grass. I knew long before I got to it that it contained the remains of a man.

Dignity in death is a civilized invention. There is no place for it in the wilderness. What Lives Again's braves had started in their superstitious determination to handicap a despised enemy on his way to the Happy Hunting Ground, the wolves, coyotes, and carrion birds had finished. But for his clothes I would not have recognized Aintchell, the former prison guard mortally wounded in his attempt to overpower Mike McPhee just before the Indian attack. My stomach crawled, but it did not turn over. Scant weeks before — even days — it might have; but the boy who had wept for his mother that same day could spare no bile for the dead in a place where all his energy was required to keep from joining them. Still, I whispered a prayer for Aintchell's soul. He had been true whatever his motives, and it seemed unlikely that Deacon Hecate had had time to do as much for him.

A wider search disclosed another heap of bones and sinew whose soiled and tattered garments I identified as those of Mike McPhee. Someone, either an Indian or one of my own retreating party, had relieved the corpse of its weapons, even going so far as to pluck Aintchell's knife from between its ribs. The skull grinned through gristle that had been the Irishman's face.

For his soul I wasted not a breath.

Everywhere were signs of upheaval: torn grass, trampled brush, rusty patches where men had bled. My head ached and I sought to relieve the pressure by unwinding Mad Alice's bandage, wincing when it tore away from the gouge in my right temple. I touched the spot gingerly. It was roughly two inches in length and formed a perfect groove. I have it still, also the headache whenever rain threatens.

The light was going. I left off the investigation to comfort my companion. He had ceased babbling and I thought at first, with a shameful mixture of grief and relief, that

I had lost him. But when I placed the back of my hand against his lips and waited, I felt his breath, faint and hot with fever. He was clinging to life as desperately as his people had fought to keep their land. I made my bed next to his and huddled close to keep him warm, for I knew something about shock — a legacy of Mother's infatuation two years earlier with a boarder who had left medical school to practice veterinary science, badly.

I did not sleep. The air was biting cold and hunger was a feral thing clawing my stomach from inside. I heard the rustling of wildlife and wondered if the scavengers that had ravaged the remains of Aintchell and McPhee would return for us. Among these considerations wound the mystery of what had become of Mr. Knox and Judge Blod and the Deacon and all the rest. It was as if a great wind had swept them from the face of the earth. Were they dead, or had the savages taken them away, wagons and all, to divide the provisions among themselves while watching the torture of their captives? After what seemed hours of this I left Panther sleeping and took a moonlight walk; as if that would induce weariness better than a full day's flight.

The sky was cloudless and the landscape

was washed in pale light. Remembering a thing that the scoundrel Black Ben Wedlock had told me, I continued in a straight line, picking out such landmarks as a shelf of fallen shale and a deformed young pine and walking from one to the next. The steady rhythm of my footsteps was mesmerizing, sponging disturbing thoughts from my mind. I even managed to forget the pain in my head.

I was planning to turn around and go back when I came out of a copse of seedling spruce and knew that I was not walking at all, and that in fact I had not left my bed beside the Indian and was asleep and dreaming.

The man who lives long enough will see many beautiful sights if he keeps his eyes open, and I imagine that I have seen most of mine. But for sheer soaring joy I cannot recall one to compare with three patched and sagging wagons arranged in a rough triangle at the base of a grassy slope not two hundred yards from the clearing where I had found the two bodies. I stopped walking and rubbed my eyes and blinked, hardly daring to do so for fear the mirage would fade. It did not, and the next thing I knew I was running.

"Mr. Knox!" I shouted, fairly flying as I

approached the wagon I knew to be his. "Judge Blod! Deacon!" From that day to this I have never felt so light and unbound by the laws of God and nature.

And then I was bound indeed.

Suddenly I was no longer running. Pain seared me as from a sudden sheet of flame, my legs flew out in front of me, and I sat down hard on the base of my spine, losing my wind and my senses. Then they returned, bringing agony with them. I could not move my arms and looked down blurredly to note that I was wrapped several times around by a strip of rounded leather, at its broadest as thick as my thumb and tapering to a frazzled tip that dangled below my chin like a visible taunt. The other end was clenched in a fist belonging to a lean man standing over me with the moon at his back so that I could not see his face. I did not need to. When he spoke, his nasal whine belonged to the demon of my nightmares.

"Well, hell," said Nazarene Pike. "It sure is scrawny, but ain't it worth keeping?" And over his shoulder: "Beacher! Fetch Black Ben."

20

Red Cloud's Medicine

Briefly I saw the face of the man whom Pike had addressed as Beacher, and recognized the bland features and sandy moustache of the man I had observed boarding our train in Denver. He said something in those melodious tones I had first heard through my window overlooking the scene of Jotham Flynn's death; then he disappeared, to return moments later in the company of that ogre of the branded face and Dresden glass eye, that fair-haired hulk who spoke of grand adventure even as he plotted mean deceit, the proprietor of the Golden Gate and keeper of the Great Lie — thief, mentor, cheat, cook, murderer, storyteller, and hound — Benjamin Franklin Wedlock. He had dressed in haste, pulling braces on over underwear, and despite the gray hairs caught in the vee of the rough cotton, the torso beneath was hard and fit. When he saw me he smiled, showing his fine teeth. It seemed to me that there was great relief in the expression; but I knew of his duplicitous heart and placed no credit in it.

"Davy, lad, we had your scalp gone by this time for sure. How'd you make away?"

"The story is as long as any of yours," I snapped, "but mine is not an insult to truth. Where are Mr. Knox and the others? What have you done with them?"

"Cheeky little bastard." Pike gave his bullwhip a vicious yank. I fell on my side.

"Let him go," ordered Wedlock.

"Little son of a bitch near got me lynched in Armadillo. I'll let him go, all right — with my saddle rope around his neck."

Wedlock drew his big Remington from his trousers and cocked it. "Pike, you're the only man I'd say a thing to more than once."

There was a short silence. Others had joined us, in varying stages of undress, including Christopher Agnes, Blackwater, and the Negro, Eli Freedman. Finally Pike cursed and let the whip go slack. The coils unwound with a hiss. I sat up, putting a hand to my pounding head.

"That's a nasty-looking crack," said Wedlock, putting away his weapon. "I got a Sioux remedy can draw the sting."

The word "Sioux" brought me back to Panther's plight. "The policeman from Standing Rock needs it more than I. I left him in the clearing where the attack took place. He is infected and feverish."

"My snakes are better company," volunteered Christopher Agnes.

Wedlock said, "Your pards was all of a piece last we seen them, Davy. Bald Jim kilt the injuns' chief and they picked up their dead and cleared off. Wasn't a minute later old Deacon Hellfire told us we had to give up our guns if we wanted to stick. Well, we was sort of unbalanced with McPhee cold as wet rock; but then Pike and Beacher showed on the high ground and got the drop on the Deacon. We traded him and the others their scalps for the wagons and supplies. They're out there somewhere. If it means a thing, I don't expect they'd of folded their cards so quick if they didn't think the injuns had kilt you and carried you off to make a soup bowl out of your skull. Took their hearts out, that did; Knox's anyway. It was just a question of odds to Holy Joe, and what guts the

Judge has wouldn't fill a shot glass."

"They are all right?" I suspected the old raider of lying even in this.

"Knox nicked a finger and the Judge took a ball through his hat and after that he didn't smell so good, but they both come out ahead of Bald Jim, him with a busted collarbone from when that chief he kilt hit him with a old Henry while he was going down. We buried young Tom. That big Swede Dolly taken one in the meaty part of his leg and I don't know about Will Asper. God-wallopers like the Deacon just shed lead like boiler plate."

"You just turned them out without horses or provisions?"

"Would of, if anyone listened to me." Pike's eyes were evil in his rodent's face.

"We let Knox and the Deacon cut out their mounts and gave them tins and water. Two men to a horse and one walking should slow them down if they're admiring to run for help. I only kill men straight up, Davy."

"Like you killed Elder Sampson?"

He looked hurt. I could not help thinking that the stage had lost a consummate actor when Ben Wedlock took to banditry. "I never wanted it that way. Why a man would put gold ahead of his own skin is beyond me."

"What about Corporal Panther? Is he to die too?"

"Injuns got no business living in the first place," said Pike. "Nor fresh-mouth brats neither."

But Wedlock was rubbing his chin. "You say he's infected?"

"He is out of his head with fever."

"I might could help him. But if I do, I'll need your word you won't bolt."

Pike said, "What do we need him for? Slit his throat and let the buzzards have them both."

"The gold, you poor dumb bastard. The boy's Knox's charge. He'll give up Flynn's map to have him back of a piece."

"There ain't no map. Knox swore to it with that hogleg of yours looking him square 'twixt the eyes."

"He knew if he gave it up it was boot hill for the lot of them. The boy's another thing. These brave ones will do for someone else's life what they'd never do for their own. He'll trade."

"*That's* why you let them go!" I cried. "You thought they'd lead you to Quantrill's gold!"

He fixed me with his good eye. "It's why we're here, Davy. It's what we do. What's your answer? I got no reason to help the injun if it's no."

There was nothing for it. Every second I delayed counted against Panther. I said, "You have my word. I won't try to escape."

"What good's that?" Pike demanded. "He'll be over the hill soon as you turn your back."

"I say he won't. And the last time I looked, what I said was the way things was. How was it the last time you looked, Pike?"

They were standing close now, so that Wedlock was looking almost directly down at the rat-faced man from his superior height. However, his greater size was not what carried the moment. Pike looked away suddenly, and in that instant I felt something of what I had felt in Jotham Flynn's presence when, so long ago, I had heard the name Black Ben for the very first time. There would be no rebellion that day.

Wedlock dispatched Blackwater and Christopher Agnes in one of the wagons to bring back Panther. Rising, I followed him to the chuck wagon; where he filled a tin cup from the water barrel and handed me a hard cake the size of a saucer. It was both grainy and greasy to the touch.

"Pemmican," he explained. "We're keeping a cold camp. Eat it. It tastes a heap better than it feels."

I was too hungry to refuse. It crumbled in my mouth when I bit into it, a surprisingly sweet morsel comprised of animal fat and berries that seemed to melt upon my tongue. I ate the rest of it and drank off the cup's contents. He watched me, wonder in his eye.

"You was a pretty sight sitting there on the ground, Davy. We figured it was just a question of whether they took you back to make medicine bags out of your hide or the coyotes got what was left. Knox, he looked thirty years older. What happened?"

My spirits were brightened somewhat by food and Panther's rescue. In any case, I was bursting to tell the story, even if it was to a brigand. I did so, consuming another pemmican cake and cup of water in the process.

"Mad Alice," he said when I had finished. "I thought she was bones by now. The injuns said she was here when the Wise One Above built the hills. Even Red Cloud —"

"Can you really help Panther?"

He frowned. "I picked up a thing or two.

233

Depends on how far gone he is and how deep down his guts go. Set some store by him, do you?"

"He is as he represents himself," I said.

The edge in my voice was not lost upon Wedlock. "I near lost my skin for that gold in '63, lad. I paid for it with my eye and eighteen months rotting in Elmira. It's more mine than anybody's and I'll have it if it means a swap with Old Nick."

"That bargain has already been struck."

He seemed about to reply when the wagon clattered into camp bearing its injured cargo. I hurried to meet it, followed closely by Wedlock, who called for a lantern and climbed into the bed. Panther's face was skull-like in the spectral light, his eyes open but uncomprehending. His breathing was shallow. Opening the Indian's shirt, Wedlock grunted approval of my dressing and used a knife to cut it away. For some moments he inspected the wound under the lantern. Then he sat back on his heels.

"Davy, I need juniper. There's a bush on the north edge of camp. Bring me a handful of sprigs."

I did as directed, climbing in beside him to pass them over. While I was gone he had raised the chimney of the lantern, and now he laid some of the green needles in the flame. Soon a sweetish smell filled the wagon. He rubbed his hands in the smoke for some moments, then placed them, palms down, upon the open wound. He repeated this practice several times, adding more juniper to the fire each time until it was gone. Panther groaned once, but otherwise remained oblivious.

"There's a clay jug in the chuck wagon and a hide bag with something in it that looks like a white radish. Get them. Also a bowl."

Locating the items in the dark of the sheeted wagon was difficult, but finally I reported back with them. He set aside the bag and poured liquid from the jug into the bowl. "This here's tea brewed from tree mold. I don't know why it works, but I seen it drag a man from hell more than once." He heated the bowl until the pungent odor of its contents mingled with the juniper still in the air. At his direction I supported the back of Panther's head while he brought the bowl to the Indian's lips and forced him to drink. More liquid spilled over his chin than inside his mouth, but I saw his throat work twice. Finally Wedlock set down the bowl, pulled the pale root out of its bag, and bit off a piece.

After chewing it for several minutes he leaned over Panther and spat directly into the wound.

The Indian took in his breath with a whine. His back arched, then settled. He grew quiet. Wedlock put his ear to Panther's chest and listened. I held my breath. After a long time he sat back on his heels again.

"He's resting now. You should too. I'll kick you up if there's a change."

"Aren't you going to dress the wound?"

"Not just yet. It needs draining."

"Will he make it?"

"That's up to him and whoever he says his prayers to."

I did not realize how desperately tired I was until I stepped down from the wagon. Automatically I fell into a habit I had not practiced since before the Indian attack: In a trance I retrieved my blanket roll from the chuck wagon, spread it out on the ground beneath, and was asleep almost before my head touched the blanket.

I awoke with Ben Wedlock's nightmare face very close and his hand shaking my shoulder. I sat up quickly, nearly banging my sore head on the underside of the wagon.

"Is it Panther?" I asked quickly.

"He's steady, lad. He'll see morning. I and Blackwater and Eli are off to talk to Knox and the others about that trade. I figured you'd want to be awake in case the injun comes around. I'm holding you to your word, now."

"My word will do that."

He smiled at my irritation. "Sure it will. I been pardnering with cutthroats so long I near forgot what it's like dealing with a gentleman. Er, I'll need your jacket. It's my bony fidey."

"Why not just take me along?"

"I can trust Knox not to fire on a white flag, but I don't know about the rest. You could pick up a bullet. Also I don't trust Pike alone with the injun. He's got a black on for the whole tribe."

"Then why not take him?"

"He goes where Charlie Beacher goes, and Beacher's looking after Bald Jim. He used to patch us up under Bloody Bill. After me he's the nearest thing to a sawbones for a hundred miles. Fetch him if anything goes wrong with the injun."

I wriggled out from under the wagon and took off my jacket. I was aware of a pair of mounted men waiting on the edge of the shadows, whom I assumed were Eli and Blackwater; also, on foot nearby, the thin wicked presence of Pike. Taking the wrong meaning from my involuntary shudder, Wedlock gave me his own blanket. As he helped me draw it on over my shoulders, he pressed something hard and slippery into my hand. My finger curled around the curve of a trigger guard.

"I'd not trust Pike at a distance of three feet," he whispered. "Remember your promise."

And then he was away, mounting his great sorrel with its damning white blaze now fully exposed to the moonlight. Turning the beast, he looked young and whole, a tower against the sky. In a moment the three were gone, and to all intents and purposes I was alone with Nazarene Pike.

21

Night of the Nazarene

Pike said nothing, although I could feel his eyes upon me from the place where he stood with the pines looming dark behind him. He was thinking, I knew, of that day at the Golden Gate Saloon, where I had denounced him as bandit and killer and very nearly proved his undoing. Presently he turned and withdrew, making almost no noise at all in the light underbrush. I tucked the pistol inside my belt and turned in the opposite direction to see to Panther. I nearly collided with Christopher Agnes.

A grin rippled his cherub's face. "Don't wake the snakes, boy. They get up ornery."

I glanced down at the burlap sack in his hand and recoiled from it. "Why do you collect the nasty things?" I asked. "There is no place to sell them out here."

"Man needs pets." From the sack he pulled a rattler as thick as his wrist, and gripping it tightly behind its head, kissed its squat snout. A black tongue fluttered out, then vanished. "Look at him. Old Christopher Agnes's throat all that's on his mind. Dreams about it, I'll warrant. You think snakes don't dream, boy? Fat mice and warm rocks, that's what they dream about. And Christopher Agnes's throat. I expect I got a reputation amongst snakes."

"I would not doubt it." I was afraid to move. I had seen one snake escape his clutches and I was well within striking distance.

At length he thrust it back inside the sack. He looked at me then, and it seemed to me that his own small eyes were reptilian in his round face.

"Think old Christopher Agnes is crazy, don't you, boy? Man likes snakes, he got to be. Well, it's like this here: "You can trust a snake to bite, on account of that's why he's on this here earth. With a man you don't always know. Yes sir, you can trust a snake not to be trusted. Remember who told you that, boy."

He walked away, humming to himself — or perhaps it was to the loathsome creatures in the sack.

I shuddered again and climbed into the wagon where Panther was resting, clutching the blanket around my throat. He did not stir when I lit the lantern, but he appeared to be breathing more evenly than before, although his color had not improved. I adjusted his own blanket and left him.

That was Judge Blod's old wagon. Mr. Knox's contained Beacher and Bald Jim, who had been wounded during the Indian attack. I went over there and pulled aside the flap. A hammer clicked in the darkness.

"It is I, David Grayle," I said quickly. "How is he?"

"He's got a hole in him; how'd you be?" The familiar voice was deceptively pleasant.

"Who is it?" I recognized these sleepy tones as Jim's. He did not sound like a man who ate Indians.

"The brat."

"What's he want?"

I said, "I wondered if you needed anything."

This time I heard a grin in Beacher's words. "Yankee gold."

I replaced the flap. Mention of the gold reminded me of Flynn's map in the pouch in my pocket. I wondered if Mr. Knox would have the presence of mind to play along with Wedlock's assumption that it was in his possession. If the bandits found out it was already among them . . .

A pair of corded hands clamped onto my shoulders from behind and tore me away from the wagon. I smelled chewing tobacco and unwashed flesh. "You little son of a bitch, I'll teach you to come slanching around men!" A boot hooked my ankle. I sprawled forward.

Twisting, I fell on one shoulder and rolled over onto my back, tugging the big revolver out from under my belt. I fired just as Pike was sliding his coiled whip off his right shoulder. He roared, rocked back on his heels, and clapped a hand to his left side, nearly dropping the whip. I pulled back the hammer a second time. The whip uncoiled then. Suddenly my hand was empty and stinging.

"I'll lay you open!" shrieked Pike.

I threw an arm in front of my face. The lash wrapped itself around my wrist and forearm, burning like flame. He tore it loose, carrying away flesh with it, and reached back to slash at me again.

"Pike! Black Ben says let him be!" Christopher Agnes lunged up behind him, catching Pike's arm in his free right hand.

The other still clutched the sack. Pike tore free and slashed at him instead. Backpedaling, Christopher Agnes stumbled and dropped the sack. Half a dozen long black glittering bodies untangled themselves from the burlap. "My snakes!"

I caught a glimpse of a terrified Christopher Agnes whirling and twisting with snakes trailing like tentacles from his arms, legs, and torso, and then I was on my feet and running, leaving the blanket behind. Pike's whip cracked. Something stung me between the shoulder blades and my shirt parted as if a razor had been drawn through it. I plunged into the columns of pines. Footsteps pounded behind me.

Thick branches above me blocked out most of the moonlight, and for a panicky moment I was in pitch blackness. I stopped to avoid a collision. The silence of that cathedral growth played tricks with my hearing; Pike's footfalls, deadened somewhat by the carpet of needles, seemed to echo all around me. I fancied I could hear his labored breathing. As my eyes adjusted, I began to pick my way between the trunks. To my ears I was making as much noise as an elk crashing through heavy brush.

Instinctively I made my way toward the

light, and eventually found myself in another clearing at the rock-strewn base of a great cliff that rose before me into darkness. Staring up at its moonlit face, I had an eerie sensation of having seen it before. A faint sound behind me in the pines helped me make up my mind. I began to climb.

The route was seductive, presenting a gentle slope at first, studded with rocks arranged in a kind of natural staircase. Soon, however, it began to steepen, the footing to turn to rubble that sank and shifted beneath my weight, slowing my progress. And then I was climbing almost straight up, curling my fingers around slippery crags and feeling with my feet for ledges no wider than a steel rule. The granite looked white under the moon. I had never felt so thoroughly exposed.

Below me, a sudden clatter of dislodged rubble followed by a curse inspired me to quicken my pace. Pike was continuing the pursuit.

The rock was cold and so was I. Very soon my fingers grew numb. Once, imagining that I had a secure handhold, I started to pull myself up to the next level, lost my grip, and slid two yards, scraping my chest and cheek and taking most of the flesh off both palms, before my right foot caught in a fissure and I stopped with a sickening lurch. I wanted to stay there, hugging the wall and listening to my heart beat. Instead I reached up with one bloody palm and started climbing once again, grateful for the stinging that allowed me to feel the features in my grasp.

I know not how long I continued to climb. My clothes were sweat through despite the cold, and clung to me clammily. I was in pain from my head injury and the blood on my hands made them slippery. I have lost track of how many times my grip failed me. I was desperately tired and sore in every limb.

Recalling stories I had heard about men and women trapped in high places, I determined not to look down — and so looked down often, only to jerk my gaze away in a fresh paroxysm of dizziness upon glimpsing the forest of sixty-foot pines from a height that made them resemble a bed of grass, and, on the expanse of steep rock that separated me from their jagged tops, scrambling spiderlike in my wake, the hatless grinning angular figure of Nazarene Pike. Dizzy I was indeed, and not just because of the altitude; for I realized that I was living my recurrent nightmare. This time it was real.

There came a point where I could climb no higher. My fingers were cramped, my own weight like lead to my overtaxed muscles. I had attained a ledge above which the wall bulged obscenely, presenting neither hand- nor foothold, and erosion had begun to disintegrate the ledge; shards of shale and broken granite shifted beneath my feet. Behind and below me I heard the breath leaving Nazarene Pike's lungs in little triumphant explosions. When I dared to look down, I saw moonlight glittering on the blood on his shirt and the hideous, gold-toothed grin of my dark dreams spreading over his ratlike face. He had lost his bullwhip, but before I could congratulate myself upon that pass, he snaked a hand behind his head, and when it came forward, the broad blade of a knife as long as my wrist caught the light.

"See old Pike strung up, would you, boy?" he panted. "Soon as I'm through gutting you like a catfish I'll go back and do your injun friend." With his free hand he groped at the ledge where I stood.

It crumbled. He slid with a gasp, clapping the hand holding the knife against the rock to catch himself. The blade scraped sparks off the granite. Then his foot found a purchase and he stopped.

"Thought you lost old Pike, didn't you, boy?" He commenced to pull himself back up.

I waited until he was reaching again for the ledge. As he curled his fingers around it I raised my right foot and brought it down hard on the ledge. A shower of pebbles pelted his face. He cursed, turned his head to protect his eyes, and fell back to his previous perch. This time, before he could resume his advance, I kicked the ledge again. More pebbles fell, then a larger shard the size of a man's hand. Then the slide started.

The entire base of the ledge was a network of cracks where moisture had frozen and swollen, weakening the stone. Now they yawned, tipping out pieces ranging in size from marbles to melons, which in their descent dislodged bigger sections farther down until the entire face of the cliff below my feet fell in thunder. I held on tight, for the very rock was shaking. Stones bounded off Pike's shoulders and grazed his head, carrying with them clouds of dust that choked him when he opened his mouth to scream. I saw him slide, catch himself, and then, as the cliff collapsed, I caught one final glimpse of his distorted, dust-caked face before he joined the avalanche. Seconds after he had vanished, I thought I could still hear his shrieks under the rumbling of the rocks settling at the base of the wall.

Any victorious emotions I might have felt would have to wait; for the very rockslide that had removed his threat had left me with no way to go but up, and as the dust settled, it was all too apparent that the bulge that had impeded my progress had not been altered one whit by the calamity. I had neither the strength nor the leverage to get over it, while below me those features that had allowed me to climb this far had been eradicated. In a phrase, I was trapped.

Nazarene Pike had been in his impromptu grave full ten minutes before I decided to move. To my right, the ledge upon which I stood existed no longer, having peeled away along with the cliff below. I made a half-hearted attempt to grasp at a handhold above me, but I was physically unable to pull myself up another inch, let alone dangle by my ruined hands for the length of time necessary to surmount that outcrop. Instead I began working my way left.

I shuffled my feet inches at a time, steadying myself with palms flat against the wall. This time I succeeded in my determination not to look down, choosing instead to feel the path with my feet. Fresh pieces of support collapsed beneath them, and in several places there were gaps, some so wide I was certain I had run out of road. At these times I came perilously close to giving up and letting go. Then my toe would catch on something solid and I would find the strength to follow it. Once, after perhaps two yards during which the ledge appeared to be broadening without a break, I hastened my pace and stepped into nothing. It was some time after I caught myself before I was steady enough to continue. If I have a reputation now for great patience, it is because nothing I have lived through since has ever seemed as long as that night suspended high over the forests that gave the Black Hills their name.

In my close concentration I had not noticed when the shadows began to recede. I was astonished upon looking up to see a sky that was more gray than black stretching beyond the top of the cliff. I was equally astonished to see that there *was* a top, and — miracle on earth! — that the way to it was a definite incline, pocked with lovely holes and jagged features for grasping and no obstacles in sight. I had circumnavigated that evil bulge entirely. Freedom was but a twenty-foot climb.

But, Jesus God, how much longer twenty feet had become within the space of a few hours.

Today I lose my patience with myself often, particularly when I find myself unable to free my middle-aged bulk from a deep sofa without indulging in elaborate vocalizations. Upon these occasions I shame myself with the memory of that boy who scaled a mountain at an age when others were attempting to master the intricacies of pedaling a bicycle. Hand over hand, foot over foot, I hauled myself up that promontory, stopping to rest often, but always returning to the task at hand. My joints were afire and I could hear, as when a jar or a conch is held to one's ear, my blood singing in my veins. At long, long last, I grasped the cliff's mossy top edge in both hands and pulled my chin up over it. There I stared at the square toes of a pair of very scuffed brown riding boots.

"You got stones, kid," said their owner pleasantly. "It's too damn bad I got to blow them off, 'specially for a scum-sucker like Pike. But a pard's a pard."

I looked up. The man's face was in shadow, but his outline, voice, and the large-bore revolver he was pointing at me all belonged to Charlie Beacher, who had sat a strawberry roan at the scene of Flynn's murder and with Pike had followed our party at a safe distance until the time came to strike. I had the crazy relieved thought that I was dreaming after all; I could not think how he had managed to get there from the camp without climbing past me.

He seemed to read my thoughts. "You boys taken the hard way. They's a nice trail winds cow-gentle up the back of this here peak."

In that moment, whatever seasoning I had acquired during that dreadful climb dropped from me, and the child that I was screamed inside my brain: *It isn't fair!* Dangling as I was from the precipice, eyes burning with tears of anger and frustration, I could not raise even a hand to defend myself against the weapon, whose cylinder was already turning as he depressed the trigger.

The report was loud and ringing, its noise alone nearly enough to jar me from my perch. Certain that I had been shot, I could not at first understand the sudden contortion of Beacher's body, hunched with the pistol rotating slowly out of his grip, until he crumpled to the ground on top of it with his hat cocked comically over one ear and his features twitching within inches of mine. Only then, in the dizzy euphoria of realizing that it was not I whom the bullet had found, did I turn my head and look down — miles down, it seemed, to the edge of that toy forest — to see Corporal Panther standing straight and tall, with Joe Snake's Winchester carbine snug to his shoulder. A patch of gray smoke scudded sideways from the muzzle in the morning wind.

22

The Trade

I have lost most of the details of what happened next. I remember pulling myself up and over the edge of the cliff — laughably easy it was, in the rush of my relief — and cooing to Beacher's strawberry roan, which, ground-hitched only and made nervous by the gunshot and the sight of the strange battered boy approaching, shied away a few exasperating yards at a time until I could seize the reins; but I do not remember at all my journey back around to where Panther awaited me. Evidently it was as gentle and uneventful a path as the dead man had claimed.

"I wish Sergeant Redfern had seen that," greeted the Indian. "He gave up trying to teach me to hit anything with a long gun beyond fifty yards."

His voice was weak. His fever had broken and he was bathed in cleansing sweat, but the effort of dragging himself from his bed and carrying the confiscated weapon through the woods had taxed him greatly. He was bleeding again.

"You should not be up," said I, dismounting.

"If I were not, you would certainly be down. I woke up alone and turned out to learn why. I followed two sets of tracks from the dead man in camp to here."

"I am grateful you did."

I relieved him of the Winchester and helped him into the saddle. This took several tries, for my legs were quivering with exhaustion. Finally he was secure and I led the roan into camp, carrying the carbine.

We were alone with Bald Jim asleep in one of the wagons and Christopher Agnes still lying where he had fallen. This time the snakes' venom had proven too much for his immunity. When I turned him over to confirm that fact, one of his killers slithered out from its warm berth beneath the corpse, buzzing its rattles. I reeled back, levered a fresh round into the Winchester's chamber, and took off its head with my second shot. Its body was still thrashing when the echo faded.

Bald Jim went on snoring.

Panther resisted my efforts to help him down. "Cut out a mount for yourself and grab some supplies," he said. "We'll need another long gun and ammunition."

I said, "You would not make ten miles in your condition."

"Leave me where I fall and ride on."

"I cannot leave this camp," said I. "I gave Ben Wedlock my word."

"The bandit?"

"Yes."

"What is the value of your word to one of his stamp?"

"It has the value I place upon it."

He regarded me. "Who is your father?"

"I never knew him. I was raised by my mother."

"I would meet her."

"If you stop at the Good Part Boarding House in Panhandle, you most certainly will."

He dismounted then, waving me off when I stepped in to assist. When he was on the ground he allowed me to help him to the chuck wagon, where I lowered the gate to make him a seat. Inside the wagon I found alcohol and proper bandages. I cleaned and dressed his wound with the efficiency of practice, noticing in the process that the unhealthy flush had faded from the skin around the gash. So there was something to Wedlock's Sioux remedy after all! But if I accepted that, then his fanciful tales of life as Chief Red Cloud's prisoner and honored guest must also be examined in a fresh light. And if he was not all lies and treachery, then how much of what he said could be kept or dismissed? I could not fathom the man.

"What now?" asked Panther. "You appear to be the clearer-headed."

I thrilled to this declaration of faith; then considered the question. "The sun is up. Wedlock and the others will return soon. They will not expect us to have overpowered Pike, Beacher, and Christopher Agnes."

"How shall we take advantage of that?"

I told him. The plan had taken vague form in my mind during the trip through the woods into camp; now the finer details worked themselves out in the telling. When I had finished, the Indian studied me again.

"You are a white man through and through, to be that devilish," said he.

"I have not lacked for examples on this journey. We must make ready."

The sun had cleared the tallest of the

hills when three horsemen appeared at the north end of camp. I recognized Wedlock in the middle aboard his blaze, with Blackwater chewing his omnipresent cigar at his right and the Negro wrangler with the withered arm at his left. I was seated on the front of the wagon where Wedlock had treated Panther, doing my best to appear bored and morose. When he saw me he halted, putting a hand up for the others to do the same. The sun flared off his glass eye when he turned it to put his good one on me.

"Where's the others?" he called.

I said, "Pike's asleep and Beacher's with Bald Jim. Christopher Agnes is out hunting snakes."

"A while ago we heard shots."

"That was Pike practicing his marksmanship."

"Funny time for it."

"He was trying to scare me," I said.

Blackwater laughed nastily. "That's Pike all right."

For a long time the trio remained unmoving while their horses, tired and smelling camp, fidgeted impatiently.

"How's the injun?" Wedlock asked then.

"There has been no change."

He scratched the blackened part of his

face. Then he raised his voice. "Beacher! Pike!"

I said, quickly, "I am worried about Panther. Will you look at him?"

Wedlock nodded at Eli and Blackwater, who started their horses toward the other wagons. The one-eyed man came my way. Abreast of me he drew rein.

"You look worse used than the last time I seen you."

"I have been up all night worrying about the Indian." The others had almost reached the wagon containing Bald Jim and no one else.

"Pike give you a hard time?"

"I have not run off," I reminded him.

After a moment he continued to the back of the wagon. I got off and circled behind him on foot. Just as he reached for the flap, Bald Jim's voice called from the wagon where he had been fast asleep.

"Beacher? Beacher, where the hell are you? I need a sip of that tanglefoot. Beacher?"

Wedlock leaned back swiftly, drawing the big Remington from under his belt. Just then Panther tore aside the wagon flap from inside and thrust the Winchester at him, working the lever for emphasis. At the same time I took the heavy short-barreled revolver out of my shirt and thumbed back the hammer. I had found it not far from where Pike's whip had snatched it from my hand.

"You're pinned tight," Panther advised him. Crouched in the wagonbed with the carbine's stock against his cheek, he looked like an Indian in a posed photograph. There was nothing artificial about his expression.

The old guerrilla froze with his pistol half drawn. "You forgot about Eli and Blackwater."

"Call them over," said Panther.

Wedlock grinned. The Indian moved the Winchester an inch and repeated the order.

"This way, boys."

They started over, leaving Bald Jim's wagon. "Ben," said Blackwater, "Beacher ain't —" He saw me holding a pistol on his leader. Out came a huge Colt's Peacemaker with the front sight filed off.

"Tell him to get rid of it!" Panther snapped. "Yours too."

Wedlock threw his weapon aside. "Do it," he said. "You too, Eli. We got us a thing here."

They hesitated. I made elaborate threatening motions with my weapon. It occurred to me then in a flash of belated wisdom that these cutthroats might care nothing for their leader, that I had made the dreadful mistake of assigning Christian motives to animals. While I was considering the implications, Blackwater cursed and let his Peacemaker drop to the ground. Eli slid a long rifle of unknown manufacture out of his saddle scabbard and threw it in the dirt.

I must have sighed audibly, because Wedlock chuckled. "Who done for Pike, the injun?" Although he was facing Panther, the question was directed at me.

"He killed Beacher. I killed Pike."

"Hell you did!" said Blackwater. " 'Less'n you back-shot him."

"Tha's how I'd do it," Eli said.

"Christopher Agnes?" Wedlock asked me.

"Killed by his pets. We buried him."

He laughed. The sound of his mirth chilled me to my soles.

"Davy, you are a one. I rode with men twice your age didn't —"

"Don't say it!"

Everything that had gone bitter inside me, all the betrayal and crushed innocence and on top of them the ordeal of the past twelve hours, had come out in those three words. He sobered.

"We had us a deal, me and you," he said. "You gave your word on it."

"Do not speak of honor to him," warned Panther. "He has more of it at his young age than you will ever know. I should hand you over to Lives Again. You will know justice before you die."

"Lives Again is dead for good. And this here's between me and Davy."

"He is right," said I. To Wedlock: "The understanding was my freedom for the map." I drew out the leathern pouch with my free hand and tossed it past him. It landed beside his horse's forefeet.

"What's that?"

"Orrin Peckler's directions to where the gold is hidden. The directions you killed Flynn to get."

"You had them right along?"

"I would have shared my portion with you." My eyes were stinging. "I would have given you all of it to go away with you and fight Indians and bandits and ride through the West like the heroes in Jed Knickerbocker's books. All you had to do was ask."

For a long time he was silent. The back of his neck was creased and red and I was aware for the first time of the deep furrows

261

on the good side of his face. He looked his age and more.

"I reckon you'll be holding us for Knox and the rest. They're due here at noon for the trade; that schoolteacher never gave up a flicker when I laid it out. Deadwood ain't far. We can be tried and strung up proper there."

"Take the map and go."

Even Panther was startled. I think that if all three of them had whipped their horses at that moment he would not have been able to collect himself in time to stop them. But they were as stricken as he.

"They are killers," he said. "You told me yourself they murdered the man Sampson."

"There is nothing to prove he did not fall from his horse and hit his head when his cinch broke. I do not care to see any of them again. The map is yours," I told Wedlock. "You are welcome to it and all the misery it has brought me. Take it and go."

He scooped it off the ground without dismounting, grunting as he straightened. He dug out the Confederate note, studied the addenda, and took off his campaign hat to fold the map inside the sweatband, throwing away the empty pouch. His fair hair was plastered tight to his big skull. His eye caught me.

"It ain't over, Davy. Someday we'll do all them things you said. The frontier ain't over for those of us with sand in our craws. Not by a damn sight it ain't." He put on the hat at a rakish angle and gathered his reins. "Let's ride, boys. We're burning daylight."

"What about our guns?" Blackwater was plainly unaware of the boon that was theirs.

"We'll get better ones and provisions in Deadwood. You'll see to Bald Jim?" he asked me. "He's a fair healer and wants for nothing but whiskey."

"We will deliver him to the authorities in good fettle. His bravery may spare him the gallows."

"Right and good!" said he; and regarded me one last time, Judas eye glittering. "No, sir, Davy. It never will be over for our kind."

He backed the sorrel away from the wagon and reared it as he wheeled. A smack of his hand on its rump and they were away, trailing the others. The trees took them in, and soon even their hoofbeats were gone.

I never saw any of them again except in dreams.

"Thank you for not interfering," I told Panther.

"You were the wronged party." Winchester lowered, he was gazing after the departed company. "And I suppose I owe Wedlock for my life. I do not know that I agree with the price."

"I have known little but wickedness since the map came into my possession. I am free for the first time in many weeks."

Wedlock for once was true to his word. The sun was barely overhead when five men entered camp from the north, two mounted, three on foot. There was no mistaking the Deacon's granite angular figure aboard his rangy claybank, or the big Swede Dahlgren riding Mr. Knox's mare Cassiopeia with a stained bandage knotted around his right thigh. Mr. Knox was leading the mare — unshaven and obviously exhausted, but no less Mr. Knox. Young Will Asper looked fit, if disgruntled. Several steps behind them hobbled Judge Constantine Blod, leaning heavily upon his stick, his overabundance of flesh hanging from him like some enforced burden. He alone was not carrying a weapon.

At sight of me, Mr. Knox uttered the only blasphemy I had ever heard from his lips and hastened forward, dropping the mare's reins so that it halted. He put away his pistol to rest his hands on my shoulders. I noticed then that one of his fingers was bandaged several times around.

"David! Lad, I thought it was another of Wedlock's tricks. When he handed me your jacket —"

"I am all right," said I; and being with him again filled me with energy, so that I told him everything, beginning with Mad Alice and finishing with Wedlock's departure, as an excited boy tells his father all the details of a day at the circus. His reactions to our escape from the stable and to the deaths of Christopher Agnes, Nazarene Pike, and Charlie Beacher were nothing compared to his astonishment over what I had done with Flynn's map.

"Gave it to Wedlock? David, what could you have been thinking? I know you were shaken, and yet —"

"That was the condition for my release," I said. "I could do no other, having given my pledge."

Will Asper was enraged. "We risk our skins and he gives the swag away like a bloody saint! Dolly and me throwed in with the wrong side!"

The Swede said something in his native tongue that did not sound like argument.

"Treasures to Babylon." Hellfire squirmed in the Deacon's ice-blue eyes. "May Elder Sampson sit in judgment."

Judge Blod was weary. "I said at the start the boy should stay home. In one fell swoop he has rendered the entire expedition meaningless."

"How can that be," said Mr. Knox wryly, "when you have said that you are not interested in wealth, only in journalistic fodder? You have made a man's choice this day, David. Your life is worth more than bullion."

"But I did not give up the bullion."

Silence surrounded me. I felt the scrutiny of six pairs of eyes. I did not keep their owners waiting.

"The map," I said, "is a lie. Follow me and I will take you to Quantrill's gold."

23

Our Quest Ends

From a distance, the stable and dugout looked like natural features of the landscape, between which the shadows of the five wooden crosses joined to form a latticework in the late-afternoon light. There was no sign of the old woman.

"It looks abandoned," said Mr. Knox, handing me his binoculars. "Perhaps she cleared out after your escape."

I focused the lenses on the stable. We had stopped the wagon containing the prospecting equipment atop a rocky knoll with an unobstructed view of Mad Alice's homestead a quarter of a mile away. With us, mounted, were the Deacon, Will Asper, and Panther on a borrowed horse. Judge Blod lay in the wagonbed complaining of his gout, which he had at last stopped referring to as a wound of honor. Dahlgren, trusting — touchingly, I thought — young Will to look after his interest, was back in camp resting his leg and keeping Bald Jim company.

"No, she is there." I returned the binoculars. "She has replaced the poles we removed, and I can see the horse moving about in the stable. The question is, how do we make our approach?"

"Straight on, if there is any truth in what you told me. Any other way would certainly invite a slug from her musket."

"We still might. There is no predicting her."

He studied me. "We needn't do this, David. That gold has claimed enough lives."

"It is no longer just the gold," I said. "It is the reason we are out here, and why good men have died. Besides, it is only a question of time before Wedlock and the others figure it out. I would not see that bandit and prevaricator gain. There is no good in him."

"Bandit and prevaricator, certainly. No man is evil through and through. I know for a fact that Wedlock is not."

I looked at him. For the first time I saw embarrassment cross his features.

"I am hardly inclined to speak in Wedlock's favor," said he. "However, there is no question that he was devastated when he thought you'd been killed."

"He said words to that effect, I have no doubt. He can make a rock shed tears when he is so inclined."

"There were no words involved. He and I saw you fall in the thick of the fighting. I tried to get to you, but just then the Indians made their push and we were driven back. I lost my gun when a bullet carried away part of my finger. When we could no longer see you for savages, we were certain you were lost as well. At that point Wedlock stood up."

"Stood up?"

"An old Sioux custom," said Panther, "when the battle is hopeless."

Mr. Knox continued. "In the midst of the fighting, with warriors galloping all around him firing and swinging their rifles like bludgeons, Wedlock rose with a pistol in one hand and a knife in the other and dared them to kill him. David, it was the most stirring sight I have beheld, and I saw many such during the war. It's a miracle he was not killed. It definitely was not for lack of trying on the part of the Indians, some of whom have surely died by now from the wounds he handed out."

"Did he . . . sing?"

"Sing?" He paused in confusion. "As a matter of fact — yes, he did sing. 'I'm a Good Old Rebel,' if I am not mistaken. How did you know?"

"He told me a story once. I thought at the time it was another of his lies."

"This is no lie. Ask the Deacon, who saw as much as I did."

"There is nothing in Scripture to equal it," announced that august person, folding long brown hands atop his saddle horn. "Had the heathens not retreated when their leader was slain, they would certainly have cut him down."

Mr. Knox smiled grimly. "It would have made a fine subject for one of the Judge's novels. Unfortunately, he missed it, having quit the field at the first sign of a feather."

"I observed that our guns were placed too close to one another," explained Judge Blod from inside the wagon. "I decided by changing positions to broaden our field of fire."

"He was broadening it lickety-split when I fetched him back," said Will Asper. "The fight was fit and Knox was afraid he'd trip and bust his gourd."

"In any case, when the Indians withdrew,

you were gone." Mr. Knox had stopped smiling. "We thought they had taken you with them, and since we were in no condition to pursue, we were forced to give you up for dead. The bandits made their move shortly thereafter. I must say Black Ben's heart didn't appear to be in it. Blackwater gave most of the orders until Pike and Beacher arrived. Wedlock took charge after that. From the look of him you'd have thought he was on the losing side of the mutiny. No, David, whatever else he was, he was devoted to you. Not that it will speak for him the day they finally drop him through the trap."

I felt the need to say something, but could think of nothing. Nor have I thought of anything to this day. I never got the man's measure.

It was decided that because a wagon appeared less threatening than a band of men on horseback. Will Asper and the Deacon must remain behind, also to protect our flanks in case this reasoning had not occurred to Mad Alice. After some protest, the Judge climbed out of the back and limped to a moss-covered boulder from where he could watch the proceedings through Mr. Knox's binoculars in relative comfort. Mr. Knox studied Panther thoughtfully.

"Perhaps you should stay here as well," he said. "The sight of an Indian would not be calming in view of what happened to her family."

"She knows me for a Sioux, not a Blackfoot."

"If she is as mad as you and David claim, she may not remember."

Panther considered. He had far from recovered from his brush with death; there were dark hollows under his eyes and the angle he sat his horse suggested that he was still in a great deal of pain from his wound. But Wedlock's treatment had released his stores of native strength.

"I will go," said he.

I said, "He has borne more than any of us. It is his right to see the thing through."

" 'And thou shalt make the breastplate of judgment with cunning work,' " intoned the Deacon, inspecting the chamber of his Henry rifle.

"Don't be too quick to use that," Mr. Knox said. "She is just an old woman after all."

"Let us not forget how she came to be old." But he scabbarded the weapon.

Panther said, "Let me ride in first."

Mr. Knox shook his head. "That is not the plan."

"She has shot at you once already," said I.

"She will shoot anyway. There is no good in all of us acting as targets. After she fires, it will take her a minute to reload. Your responsibility will be to get to her before she does."

"What if she does not miss the first time?" I asked.

"That is *my* responsibility."

Mr. Knox was prepared to argue and would have, had not Panther dug in his heels and bolted ahead down the slope in the direction of the dugout. I, who had the team's reins, flipped them before Mr. Knox could nudge me. We rattled off in the Indian's wake.

Despite my anxiety for Panther, who was unarmed, I felt strange returning to that place from which we had so recently fled. Although scant days had passed since then, so much had happened in the interim that it was like coming back to a seat of childhood memories. Both the stable and the dugout appeared smaller and more crude than I remembered, the distance between them shorter. Only the graves looked the same.

I saw the smoke an instant before I heard the report, blossoming raggedly inside the entrance to the dugout before the wind took it. Panther cartwheeled out of his saddle, rolled on the ground, and lay still. His horse screamed and galloped riderless straight through the yard and down toward the stream that supplied water to the site.

"Panther!" I shouted.

"I am all right! Get inside!"

Mr. Knox was off and running toward the dugout before I could set the brake. The horses ground to a halt on stiffened legs, the wheels screeched, the wagon tilted, hung, and crashed back down with a force that threw me out of the seat. I hit the ground running and tore through the flap that hung over the dugout entrance. I had to grasp the edge of the opening to keep from colliding with Mr. Knox.

As my eyes adjusted to the dimness inside, I saw the schoolteacher with his arms locked around Mad Alice, struggling to contain her as she squirmed and hissed and tried to swing the empty musket by its barrel like a club. The stock came around, snatching off my hat as I ducked. Instinctively I threw a hand up to protect my head and my fingers closed around the weapon. Acting purely upon reflex, I tore it out of her grasp.

She was by no means helpless even then. Bareheaded, hair and eyes wild, she struggled and spat and scratched like a feral cat, kicking and shrieking obscenities that she must have learned from her trappers and prospectors who had passed her way.

"Madam! Cease! Desist, I say! This will —" A small hard fist landed flush upon Mr. Knox's chin, snapping his teeth together.

Gentlemanliness was not at issue. Leaning the musket against the wall beyond her reach, I spotted the empty stewpot atop the ancient chest of drawers, picked it up by its handle, and was preparing to hit her over the head with it when Panther came in.

"Star-Touched Woman, stop," he said.

I know not what meaning the name the Sioux had given her held for her, or how Panther knew. At the time it did not matter. What mattered was she ceased struggling. Her eyes, watching the Indian, were like bright tiny sparks in her round face.

Very slowly, Mr. Knox released her and put a hand to his mouth. Her blow had caused him to bite his lip, which was bleeding copiously. He found a handkerchief and pressed it to the new wound. "You are not hit?" he asked Panther.

"I saw the musket just in time."

"Thought you'd be dead by this." In spite of her labored breathing, Mad Alice spoke as casually as a Panhandle hostess. "The boy's some doctor, I guess. Boy, you owe me a good kitchen knife."

I put down the pot. "You remember me?"

"I'm crazy. Not forgetful."

"Madam," said the schoolteacher, "my name is Henry Knox. My companions, whom I believe you have met but not by name, are David Grayle of Panhandle, Texas, and Corporal Panther of the reservation police at Standing Rock."

"I thought you was my Charlie when you come in that way. We used to have us some screamers, Charlie and me did. Redskins took him last week, my boys too."

"Your husband and sons are dead," said Panther.

Mr. Knox glared at him. "That is not the way."

Mad Alice said, "What you want? I got supper to hunt up."

"Madam, we have a proposition, if you will hear it," Mr. Knox said.

"Spit it out. I'm losing the light."

Dusk was sifting in when we emerged from the dugout. Mad Alice went immediately to the wagon while Mr. Knox waved to the others on the hill. By the time the Deacon, Will Asper, and Judge Blod joined us — the Judge riding double on the holy man's claybank — the old woman had most of the contents of the wagon strewn about the yard and was seated among them like a little girl, examining each item in turn. These included the picks and shovels we had carried along as part of our pose as prospectors, as well as sardines and sardinelles in tins, sundry fruits sealed in jars, cheese, salted meat, and a wide variety of pots and spoons and other cooking utensils borrowed from the chuck wagon. She made delighted little noises over each piece of booty and looked not at all like a local legend of forty years' standing. She became hostile only once, baring what teeth remained in her head when Mr. Knox picked up one of the shovels; then subsided back into her cooking inventory when he explained that he would return it presently.

"Which one, madam?" he asked.

"That one there, by the stable." She admired her reflection in the bottom of a measuring cup.

Mr. Knox walked to the last grave in the line of five, removed the stones from the mound, and began digging. Will Asper, who had dismounted to watch, said, "Taking up a new line of work, school-teacher?"

"She saw Peckler bury the gold at the foot of Mount Harney," said he, turning over the first spadeful. "It wasn't in the ground an hour before she dug it up and carried it here. It must have taken a dozen trips, but she knew it was worth the effort if she could use it to negotiate with the Blackfeet to return her husband and sons. How she explained to herself the presence of the first four graves, when she insisted upon believing them to be still alive, is not for me to answer; demented people are geniuses at self-delusion. Gold means nothing to Indians, however, and in time, as it laid useless in the earth, she even forgot she had it. Jarring her memory took some time. The articles in that wagon were of much greater value to someone in her position."

The ground was hard, and each of us took a turn except Panther — even Judge

Blod, who appeared to have forgotten his gout entirely. The light was almost gone when the Deacon spelled him. He had taken but one scoop when the blade of the shovel struck something that rang.

24

And Last

My tale is all but told; and yet, as maddeningly happens once one has closed and strapped his grip, I see that there are items left to pack.

The fifth grave was filled with glittering gold double-eagles, a glorious sight to boy and man. The wooden crates in which they had been buried had long since rotted away, and so we were most of the night transferring them from that dank hole to the wagon by lantern light. Mad Alice had by this time gathered up and moved her new wealth inside the dugout, where when Mr. Knox and I put our heads in to say good-bye she had pried the lids off most of the jars; unaware that this would spoil the contents within days. In an excess of pity, I thereupon left her with Joe Snake's Centennial Winchester and several boxes of ammunition for hunting purposes — hoping that she would not choose to employ them against unwitting passersby. When last I saw her she had peeled the bright label off one of the tins to decorate her flowered hat with the gay legend EMERSON'S MERMAID BRAND QUALITY SARDINES. It pleases me to think that she is still there, being spoken of in gleeful disbelief by the modern local residents and plotting schemes for the release of her family from the Blackfeet. If so, she would be considerably more than one hundred years old.

At dawn we returned to our camp, the team straining mightily against its new burden, collected Dahlgren and Bald Jim, and left for Deadwood under the guidance of the Deacon. On our way there we were intercepted by Major Alonzo Rudeen and his cavalry, our escorts on the trek from Cheyenne to the Black Hills. The major explained that he had received orders to round up Lives Again and his renegades and return them to Standing Rock and, if they refused, to compel them to surrender under force of arms. Corporal Panther identified himself and informed him that what remained of that band was likely already on its way back to the reservation. Plainly Rudeen did not believe him and our companies parted after he had shaken hands with Judge Blod, his champion in the eastern press. Somewhere in the history of that region, the reader may find reference to Alonzo Rudeen's gallant victory over Lives Again's warriors a few days later at Hot Springs. I report now that the "battle" was a slaughter of an already defeated and leaderless band bent upon surrender, and I invite Rudeen if he is still living, or any of his descendants if he is not, to challenge me in open court.

In Deadwood, which was an armed camp amidst rumors of uprising among the Ghost Dancers at Standing Rock, we received proper medical attention for Dahlgren's wounded leg, Bald Jim's broken collarbone, Panther's torn side, Mr. Knox's abbreviated finger, Judge Blod's intermittent gout, and my scraped hands and aching head. (Of our party, only the Deacon and Will Asper were unscathed — proving, perhaps, that good fortune falls to opposite extremes.) In the doctor's reception room awaiting our turns, we held a conference and agreed to say nothing to the law of Bald Jim's part in the mutiny. Whatever his past sins, which we assumed were legion, he had redeemed himself for his treachery by dispatching Lives Again, thus turning certain massacre into victory. Bald Jim was grateful in his quiet way. I have no doubt that he has since gone to judgment by way of the gun or the rope. In any case my conscience is clear on his subject.

We made no contact with the authorities during our brief stay in that city. Just as it was in Wild Bill Hickok's day, Deadwood was filled with brigands and opportunists who would think nothing of falling upon our little group as soon as we were clear of civilization and making off with the gold, and so we prevented rumors of our wealth from spreading by saying nothing of our original mission. Certain were we also that the law would do little, preoccupied as it was with the situation among the Indians. Indeed, even Major Rudeen had displayed no curiosity about our diminished numbers and obvious hard use. This was on the eve of that tragic last period in the conquest of the prairie which would end that winter in the so-called Battle of Wounded Knee.

Corporal Panther took his leave of us on our last day. He was needed on the reservation, he said, and his family was waiting for word of his safety. Because Indians were not allowed in the hotel, he met me in front of the livery where he had been staying to say good-bye. He put his hand on my shoulder.

"We have shed blood for each other," he said, "and that makes us brothers. There is room for you in my tipi if you ever tire of your civilization."

I do not recall what I said in response; something inane, I suspect. We clasped hands, and he went inside to saddle the horse we had given him. He had refused a share of the gold.

He never made it back to Standing Rock. I learned later that he was shot in the back while on his way out of the Black Hills by a white miner for his horse and rig. The federal court in Yankton acquitted the miner of murder on the grounds of self-defense. The Ghost Dance campaign was in full swing at this time.

We sold one of the wagons, repaired the others, stocked up on supplies, and struck out for Cheyenne, this time along the more direct route used by the Deadwood stage. The return journey was made without event. It seemed longer than the circumspect trip out and — Devil take an ungrateful boy — boring. I rejoiced when it ended.

Outside the city limits we stopped to divide the double-eagles. We were six, and each of us, having shared the dangers equally, received an equal part. When Mr. Knox handed me more, Will Asper bridled.

"Where's he rate?"

"David's mother was involved long before you," said Mr. Knox. "She had already earned a percentage when you came in."

"I didn't see her around when we was fighting them red bastards."

"Nor do you see her receiving payment equal to those who did. If not for her and her boarding house we would never have known of the gold's existence. We shall not argue about this further."

Morosely, Will Asper distributed his share between his saddle bags and rode out, accompanied by Dahlgren. I do not know the fate of that good-natured Swede, but it seems likely that he invested his share honestly and with generosity. Many years later I heard a rumor that Asper was killed at Veracruz, fighting as a mercenary in the pay of Pancho Villa. I often wondered, if this was true, what had become of his portion of the gold. Riches do not stay long with men of his temperament.

Mr. Knox asked Deacon Philo Hecate what plans he had for his share. "You cannot spend all of it upon stained-glass windows."

"Blast the windows! I shall build a cathedral." The preacher's voice boomed. "The lowliest sinner shall find his shelter beneath a roof of gold."

"Ezekiel?"

"Philo."

My last memory of that thunderous old man is of his gaunt frame guiding his claybank toward town at a stately pace, saddle pouches bulging with coins and Bible. In the spring of 1901, a friend who had married and moved to Wyoming sent me the following item from the obituary page of the Laramie *Record:*

Philo Heracles Hecate, aged 78, died suddenly Sunday at the House of the Blessed Lamb in Cheyenne, where he had been pastor for the past ten years. Witnesses to the tragedy, which took place during morning services in the grandiose Italian *baroque* church on Central Avenue, said Deacon Hecate suffered apoplexy near the end of his sermon and expired before anyone could come to his aid. The House of the Blessed Lamb, designed by its pastor and constructed upon the site of its modest predecessor, had been the subject of much debate between leaders of the congregation and city fathers, who would demolish it to make room for a skating parlor. Burial Tuesday following 10 a.m. services at the Schechaniah Sampson Memorial Chapel adjacent to the church.

In Cheyenne we sold the two remaining wagons and all but one horse to Sam Greenspan for less than half what we had paid him for just the wagons, and booked seats on the afternoon train to Denver with a connection to Amarillo. Mr. Knox made arrangements at a livery to board his mare Cassiopeia and send her out on the next stock train. Our identical new satchels, which required two hands to hoist on board, drew curious glances from some of our fellow passengers, but we paid them no heed.

Of the scene that occurred at Cousin Gertrude's house when my mother and I were reunited I will say little, for she has always been embarrassed by outward demonstrations of affection and may yet read these words. Suffice it to say that it felt grand to be treated as a little boy once again, to be embraced by her and even to suffer Gertrude's obfuscatory greetings and breathless comments about how many inches I had grown in such a short time. That effusive woman did not appear to notice my wrapped hands and cut head. Although neither Mr. Knox nor Judge Blod nor I made reference to our hardships, I think from the look that passed between Mother and the schoolteacher when he took her hand politely that she understood all. To this day she has not asked me for an accounting. Her reaction was much less reserved when, in the privacy of the trap Mr. Knox hired to take us back to the station, I showed her what my satchel contained. She chattered incessantly of plans for the fortune — most of which never came true, I am happy to say; for I had no desire to attend Princeton.

Judge Constantine Blod bade us all farewell at the Good Part Boarding House, where he had returned solely to retrieve his bags. There he regained enough of his customary fustian to recite the "goodnight" speech from *Macbeth*; unimpressing my mother, who had cooled toward him greatly in his absence. Anyone observing their parting might have supposed that here were a lodger and a landlady who had scarcely met during the former's stay. To me he said precisely nothing.

I confess to a feeling of bitterness toward him yet, although he has been in his grave these fifteen years, having spent his final days secluded in a mansion on San Francisco's Nob Hill said to have survived the earthquake, crippled by gout and waiting for gangrene to take him. This is an unfair attitude, for if it were not for that early exposure to the popular press of the day, I should hardly be living in relative comfort on New York City's Upper West Side, the owner of a publishing firm whose line of pulp magazines, including *Dime Dazzlers*, *Racy Detective*, *Sixgun Western*, and *Tales from the Dungeon*, is selling surpassingly well despite a rather troublesome economic slump in this year of 1930. The only one of my enterprises not doing well, and which I have consistently refused to part with in the face of my lawyer's earnest entreaties to divest, is the geriatric Progressive Publications, Inc., based in Chicago, which has been losing money for years and whose sole claim to notoriety is that it was once Jed Knickerbocker's imprint.

Henry Knox and I correspond often since he retired as superintendent of the Panhandle School District, incorporated in 1899. Although in his late seventies, he is in sound health and attends all the games played by the boys' softball team he has sponsored for years, among his many community endowments and activities. He and my mother exchange Christmas cards faithfully, which I find heartening in view of the fact that they have been divorced since 1893, eighteen months almost to the day after their wedding. (His first wife succumbed to smallpox within a month of our return from Dakota). He has been urging me for some time to write this chronicle, and I am under pain of an angry letter to send it to him before publication so that he can correct the geography.

My mother is living, as I said. She sold the Good Part soon after the divorce and long after she had ceased to require the income provided by her lodgers; her reasons for keeping it so long, I am bound to relate, were a factor in Mr. Knox's decision to end the marriage. Two years later she married a third time and resides today in Chicago with her husband, who owns and manages a chain of meat-packing plants and slaughterhouses headquartered in that city. They are active socially and last month were weekend guests in the Florida home of Mr. and Mrs. Al Capone. I make it a point to visit on birthdays and holidays and occasions when my stepfather is away on business. He and I do not get on.

This year, a sculptor named Gutzon Borglum plans to unveil a gigantic head of George Washington he fashioned by means of chisels and dynamite out of a rock cliff named Rushmore, located somewhere in the Black Hills. It is to be joined by other heads. I read an interview in which Mr. Borglum stated that he chose the site because of the friendliness of its configuration to his purpose. I felt like congratulating myself, for the photograph that accompanied the interview was certainly of the cliff I had climbed, whose contours I had created by bringing down the entire face upon the head of Nazarene Pike.

I do not know what became of Black Ben Wedlock. He never returned to the Golden Gate Saloon, and today a filling station occupies that site. I hear rumors from time to time, mostly having to do with some scoundrel's death under a variety of disgraceful circumstances, but nothing concrete. I became excited once when a manuscript arrived on my desk purporting to be the fictionalized memoirs of one Franklin Bridegroom, "hero of the boarder" (sic); handwritten in a childish scrawl and nearly incomprehensible in its spelling, grammar, and punctuation, it was peppered nonetheless with authentic details and genuine frontier aphorisms (among numerous impossible escapes, willy-nilly chases, contrived rescues, and one-man victories over absurd odds) to convince me that its author was intimate with his subject. There was no cover letter and no return address on the envelope, only a Santa Fe postmark. I brooded over this unpublishable book for weeks, hoping that whoever had submitted it would get in touch with me. When he did not, I hired a private detective based in Albuquerque, who poked around the New Mexico capital for two weeks and sent me a ten-page report detailing his failure and a bill for seventy-five dollars. I still have the manuscript, and thus far no one has come forward to claim authorship.

I think of him often, and seldom with rancor. He was as he represented himself, if not precisely what he claimed to be; and if that makes no sense, then the reader will never understand why a thirteen-year-old boy should leave a good home to treat with guerrillas and Indians in the last decade of the old century. Given that same energy and the wisdom I now possess, I should do exactly as I did; for unlike the gold, long since spent and forgotten, the memories of adventure have grown brighter each year. And sometimes they are more than just memories. Sometimes — more since the death seven years ago of my beloved wife, Natalie, than before — when I lie half-awake in that flat black quarter hour that precedes the light, I hear distinctly unmusical voices raised in song, and I swear that they are just outside my window:

Oh, I'm a good old rebel,
now that's just what I am!

And I am ready.

About the Author

Loren D. Estleman is a prolific and versatile author who, since the publication of his first novel in 1976, has established himself as a leading writer of both mystery and Western fiction. His novels include *Mister St. John*, *Murdock's Law*, *The Glass Highway*, *The Midnight Man*, *Stamping Ground*, and the winner of the Western Writers of America's 1981 Golden Spur Award for Best Historical Western, *Aces & Eights*.

The employees of Thorndike Press hope you have enjoyed this Large Print book. All our Thorndike and Wheeler Large Print titles are designed for easy reading, and all our books are made to last. Other Thorndike Press Large Print books are available at your library, through selected bookstores, or directly from us.

For information about titles, please call:

(800) 223-1244

or visit our Web site at:

www.gale.com/thorndike
www.gale.com/wheeler

To share your comments, please write:

Publisher
Thorndike Press
295 Kennedy Memorial Drive
Waterville, ME   04901